Book your adventure!

Chuna Cox

The

Ninespire

Experiment

Real heroes read!

David Anthony

Dedication

David:
Bill and Judi Beaver

Charlie:
In memory of Jim Sapp

The authors would like to express a special thanks to the Michigan Reading Association (MRA) for its continued support.

ISBN 0-9728461-6-6

Printed in the U.S.A.

First Printing, April 2006

The Ninespire Experiment
Table of Contents

1. A Long Name For Spider....................9
2. Great Ball of Fire......................12
3. Ode to a Toad..........................16
4. Moan Stones...........................20
5. Princess Oilcan.......................25
6. Tongue Tide...........................30
7. Scoot Boots...........................34
8. Look Who's Talking....................38
9. Goblin Delight........................41
10. Ugh, Ugsuds!.........................45
11. Card Tricks..........................49
12. A Hero's Heart.......................54
13. A Hole to Somewhere 58
14. Simon Little.........................63
15. Dancing Bananas......................68
16. Hocus Pocus..........................72
17. Invisible to Visible.................77
18. Happy Baby or Not....................81
19. Imposter Ast.........................85
20. Heart and Goal.......................89
21. Food Fight...........................94
22. Noble Reunion........................99
23. Wizard, Window, Witch...............103
24. Heartthrob and Broomstick...........108
25. Dead and Death.......................112
26. Diapers to the Rescue...............116
27. What Happened to AnnaBell...........120
28. Big vs. Smart.......................126
29. Peggy-sis the Pegasus...............130
30. Pop Tent Event......................134
31. A Glitch in Time....................140
32. Everything Except Mushrooms........144

33. *GROINK!*.....................................149
34. Slurp'n'Burp.............................154
35. Arachno-Hut.............................158
36. S.A.M.B.U..............................162
37. Would-be Hero..........................167
38. AnnaBell Antique.......................170
39. Dead Dead End..........................174
40. Time Stopping Time.....................178
41. Five Steps.............................182
42. Dead Stay Dead.........................186
43. One Horror For Another.................190
44. O.F.L.A.P..............................194
45. Distract For the Hat...................198
46. Bah-Bah-Boom!..........................205

Name Pronunciation Guide
for
Knightscares #7:
The Ninespire Experiment

In adventure books like Knightscares, some names will be familiar to you. Some will not. To help you pronounce the tough ones, here's a handy guide to the unusual names found in this book.

arachnoped
uh - rack - no - pedd

Mephello
Meh - fell - low

Mougi
Moo - gee

Spinasaurus Rex
Spy - nuh - soar - us Rex

ugsud
Ugg - sud

Zeila
Zee - luh

Visit www.knightscares.com to hear the names pronounced on your computer by the authors.

Tiller's Field and Surroundings

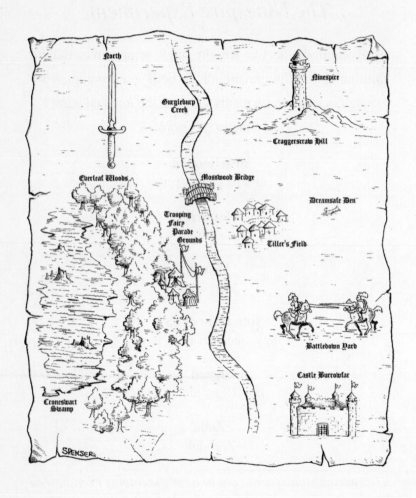

#7:
The Ninespire Experiment

David Anthony
and
Charles David

A Long Name For Spider

1

Glizzzk-thoong. Glizzzk-thoong.

Gears whirling, my arachnoped chugged uphill. Its eight spider-like legs scuttled over rocks, and I pedaled harder, eager to get where I was going.

I was on my way to see Wizard Ast and had been riding all afternoon to reach him. He lived in a tall castle named Ninespire on the top of Craggerscraw Hill. I could barely make out the dragon statue that guarded his home.

Castle Ninespire was a mysterious place. People whispered when they spoke its name or discussed its strange magic. Some folks even claimed that it was alive.

That morning I wasn't one of those people. I still thought Ninespire was like any other castle. But I was about to learn that the rumors were true. Ninespire had secrets that few people dared to imagine.

Glizzzk-thoong. Glizzzk-thoong.

9

Puffing from the effort, I continued to pedal, and my arachnoped continued to climb. Riding an arachnoped was usually fun, kind of like sitting on the back of a giant spider. But this spider had levers, pedals, gears, and a seat because it was a machine.

Almost everyone I passed turned to stare when I rode by. I smiled at them and waved like a princess in a parade.

Princess Gidget, that's me. Well, without the Princess part. I've always enjoyed getting my hands, knees, and clothes dirty too much for a real princess.

Blame that on my father. He's the tinker of Tiller's Field, my home town. He even named me after his work—*gadget* ... *Gidget*. A tinker builds gadgets like my arachnoped riding machine. Most people think my dad's gadgets are magic but they aren't.

I have brown eyes and short, curly black hair. Instead of a princess' tiara, I wore a pair of goggles on my head, a sturdy tool belt, and plain clothes. I was twelve years old and kept a slingshot in my back pocket for emergencies.

Ninespire was getting close, and I gazed at it with mixed feelings. I was eager to finish my trip, but the castle wasn't the most inviting place. Just one look at its dark walls told me to beware. All of the spooky stories could be true.

I tried not to shiver when the shadow of the castle's tallest tower fell over me. The sun had nearly set, and the brightest light came from the castle. An electric radiance pulsed around it like the steady rhythm of a beating heart.

No, Ninespire wasn't like other castles. I could almost believe that it really was alive.

"I hope Wizard Ast has dinner ready," I said out loud, trying to get my mind off the castle's eerie appearance. "Some kingbite cookies sound good—"

VLOO-OOMM!

The explosion came without warning. There was no telltale rumble in the ground. There was no smoke. One second I was pedaling hard. The next I was thrown from my seat and sent spinning downhill.

Dirt and rocks whirled in a dusty blur. Metal flashed at the edges of my vision. Then a heavy crash and the sound of screeching gears told me my arachnoped wouldn't be walking again anytime soon.

I landed hard on my back but managed to slap my goggles down over my eyes. I did it just in time, too, because blinding fire blazed before my eyes.

A roaring fireball as wide as a wagon streaked straight toward me. It hissed like a nest of angry vipers and sent fiery sparks the size of apples streaking in every direction.

There was no way I could escape. The fireball was going to plow right into me!

Great Ball of Fire

2

The fireball shrieked toward me, and I shrieked, too, expecting to die. I raised my arms uselessly and felt no hope. The end was near.

"Wizard Ast!" I wailed. "Please, somebody help!"

There was no response, of course. The wizard was far away and couldn't help or even hear me. There was no one else around. I was as alone as a girl could be.

The fireball came fast. I expected pain. I expected deadly heat and the crushing blow of a sledgehammer. But what I really got amazed me.

Nothing! The fireball zipped through me as if I were a ghost.

Z-z-z-zlip!

It struck me, I swear it did. But I felt no pain, just a tingling in my chest and belly. My hair stood up straight, and electricity crackled between my fingertips. Then the fireball was gone like a passing breeze.

I lay on the hillside for a long time, panting and wondering why I had survived. I should have been dead and turned to ash. People didn't survive being clobbered by fireballs.

But I could still feel my frightened heart thundering in my chest. *Thwoon-thwoon! Thwoon-thwoon!* I was definitely alive, and that meant something.

Aching and sore in a dozen places, I gingerly climbed to my feet. My arachnoped lay on its side a short distance away, twisted and jammed between two large rocks. Walking the rest of the way was my only choice.

So I got moving—slowly. I needed dinner more than ever. Now I needed answers, too.

Where had the fireball gone? Why hadn't it hurt me? What had Wizard Ast done to—?

Wizard Ast!

The fireball had come from Castle Ninespire, and Wizard Ast was inside. What had the explosion done to him?

Without pausing to brush the dust from my clothes, I started to run. Wizard Ast might need me. He could be alone and in serious trouble.

Clouds of dust hung in the air from the explosion. I could barely see the ground at my feet. Ninespire was just a bluish haze a short way uphill.

Rocks and holes appeared in my path without warning. They forced me to jump and zigzag like a frightened deer racing through the woods. The contents of my backpack

13

clanked as I ran.

"Don't break, please, don't break," I repeated with every clink and clunk. My backpack was filled with gadgets for Wizard Ast. They were from my father, and delivering them was my reason for visiting.

Thwoon-thwoon! Thwoon-thwoon!

Even my heart got into the noisy act. It pounded so loudly that it drowned out everything else. That was strange. I wasn't even tired yet..

I quickly stopped running and placed a hand on my chest. My heart sounded as if it was going to burst, but I could hardly feel it beating.

"Rusty buckets, Gidget," I complained out loud. "Aren't you in better shape?" Running usually didn't wear my out so easily.

Thwoon-thwoon. Thwoon-thwoon.

But my heart didn't agree. It thundered louder, hammering in my head and ears and behind my eyes. In seconds, its noise drove me to my knees.

Thwoon-THWOON!

I clutched my head in my hands and moaned. "Please, stop!"

THWOON-THWOON! THWOO—

And then there was silence.

Exhaling heavily, I pushed myself to my knees. At first I could see nothing, but a strange building slowly took shape on the top of the hill.

It was Ninespire, but not the Ninespire I remembered. Something had changed it. The explosion had done something magical to the castle.

Wizard Ast's home was now shaped like a giant frog five stories high!

Ode to a Toad

3

I scrubbed the lenses of my goggles in disbelief. Was I seeing what I thought I was seeing? Had Ninespire really been turned into a giant frog?

I crept uphill, swatting at clouds of dust. "Rusty buckets," I muttered. "This is bad." So bad that I forgot about how loud my heart had been beating.

If the explosion had turned the castle into a frog, I hated to imagine what it had done to Wizard Ast. He had already been turned into a frog once before.

As I got closer, Ninespire became clearer. To my relief, the whole thing hadn't changed. Just the statue that guarded it was different. A stone frog squatted where a statue of a dragon had crouched for many years.

The dragon's job had been to guard the castle and keep away unwanted visitors. It had done this by asking riddles. Only those who answered correctly were allowed inside.

Now I couldn't help wondering what a frog would do to try to keep me out.

"Compose thou *ribbit*-wisely," it croaked in a deep voice when I neared.

I ignored the statue and tried to peek around it. But its frog chin ballooned outward, blocking my view. I couldn't spot a door or stairway anywhere.

"A song," the frog demanded.

I froze. *A song? Compose thou wisely?* The dragon had always asked riddles, but the guardian statue was a frog now. Was it demanding that I sing?

I shrugged and sang the first thing that came to mind. I hoped no one but the frog was listening.

Keep the sugar.
Keep the spice.
Not all girls think those are nice.

Pass the hammer.
Pass the nail.
I'm at least part puppy tail.

Don't just label.
Don't just guess.
Some girls like to make a mess.

It was a silly song, I know, but it was also the one I knew best. My father taught it to me when I was very young, and I hummed it whenever I tinkered.

17

When I finished singing, I glanced anxiously at the frog. Its chin ballooned outward again and it croaked.

"Ribbit-wrong," it declared. "Two chances more. Compose thou wisely."

"Figures," I grumbled. I should have known a nursery rhyme wouldn't be enough. Solving the dragon's riddles had always been tough. Composing a song for the frog probably would be, too.

Wait! That was it. *Composing a song.* The frog didn't want me to sing a song I already knew. It wanted me to make one up. That's what composing is—writing.

I trotted away from the frog and started to pace. Pacing helps me think whenever I'm stumped. A great title for my song popped into my head right away and I giggled.

Ode to a Toad.

Technically, frogs and toads were different, but I hoped that wouldn't matter. Funny should count for something, right?

The actual words to the song took longer to compose. I was good at fixing things and building things and getting dirty, not at writing. But I decided to work on that. Everyone has to write once in a while. It's important to be good at it.

After finishing, I walked back to the frog and cleared my throat. This time I really hoped no one was listening.

"Ode to a Toad," I announced formally, but the frog didn't flinch. Not even its chin puffed out.

Tough crowd, I thought as I started to sing.

Oh, how I like to hop from here to there,
Leaping, springing, sweeping through the air.

Oh, how I like to croak from deep down low.
Grumble, ribbit, rumble—hear me go.

Oh, how I like to sing a warty ode—
Rhyming, chanting, chiming for a toad.

Oh, how I like to hop …
Oh, how I like to croak …
Oh, how I like to sing *Ode to a Toad*!

I finished, panting for air. I wasn't much of singer, and hitting the right notes had been a challenge.

Vvv-lup!

Before I could catch my breath, the frog opened its mouth and fired out its whip-like tongue. I leaped sideways, but the tongue was too fast.

Splurp! It slapped against my waist, coiling around and around. The tongue was sticky and wet and as rubbery as an octopus' arm.

I wanted to scream but gagged instead. Yuck! This wasn't the kind of mess I enjoyed.

Then the tongue gave a firm tug and started to drag me toward the frog's open mouth. I managed to scream just before the olive lips parted wide enough to swallow me whole.

Moan Stones

4

Sweaty. That was how it felt inside the frog's mouth. Sweaty and muggy like a swamp during a thunderstorm.

Sticky darkness surrounded me. Heavy, moist air filled my lungs. I wanted to scream but was afraid to take a deep breath. I could have drowned!

Rib-blurp!

The frog opened its mouth, flicked its tongue, and let out a disgusting wet burp. The force sent me flying into clean, fresh air.

Clarng! Tarng! Thurnk!

I crash-landed on a stone floor, metal gadgets clanking. Whizmos spilled out of my backpack, and a drivet poked uncomfortably into my back. Those were some of the gadgets I was supposed to be delivering to Wizard Ast.

Even lying in a tangle on the floor, I'd never felt so relieved. I was out of the frog's mouth and inside Castle

Ninespire. Now I could find Wizard Ast and some dinner.

With a grimace, I rolled over and scooped up my whizmos. Thankfully none of them was damaged, and neither was I. Wizard Ast wouldn't want broken gadgets. I didn't want a broken Gidget.

I stood in an empty round room that looked like a tower. Stone walls without windows crowded around me, rising high above. With my arms stretched straight out from my sides, I could touch them with both hands at the same time.

"Anyone home?" I called into the air, trying to sound brave. There was something odd about the tube-shaped room. Something that had nothing to do with its shape.

Then I got it. The room didn't have a door.

A deep, breathy voice groaned nearby, prickling the hairs on the back of my neck.

"*Who-oo-oo go-o-oes there?*" it moaned. It sounded like a ghoul hissing in a graveyard.

I spun around, trying to spot who or *what* had spoken. The room was still empty, but the walls seemed closer together.

"*W*-who said that?" I stammered, forgetting about being brave.

Taunting laughter boomed throughout the room, coming from everywhere at once. It rattled my teeth and vibrated in my chest.

"*Mwa-ha-ha-ha! We are the mo-o-o-oan sto-o-o-ones!*" This time the voice didn't sound like a single ghoul. It sounded like dozens of them. *"Mo-o-o-oan sto-o-o-ones!"*

I covered my ears and continued to spin. I'd never heard of moan stones before, and I thought I'd seen everything in Ninespire. Simon, Wizard Ast's apprentice, had even shown me secret passages and laboratories filled with bubbling potions.

Why hadn't he shown this room to me?

"Mo-o-o-oan sto-o-o-ones!"

The moan stones roared with wicked laughter, and I racked my brain for an answer. If I didn't keep thinking, I'd scream. The walls felt as if they were creeping closer. The voices were definitely louder.

The explosion! I thought suddenly. *Maybe it did something to the whole castle, not just the statue outside.*

Something dangerous was going on. Explosions, fireballs, frog statues, and moan stones didn't just appear out of nowhere. There was a mystery here that needed to be solved.

I squared my shoulders and glared at the wall. It didn't matter which wall. The moan stones were everywhere.

"I want to see the wizard," I demanded, hoping to sound brave again.

"The wonderful wizard?" a high-pitched voice cackled insanely. The other moan stones giggled wickedly.

"No-o-o-o wizards he-e-e-ere! O-o-only witches!"

Witches? First ghouls, now witches. Had Ninespire been turned into a haunted house? I almost expected to hear the

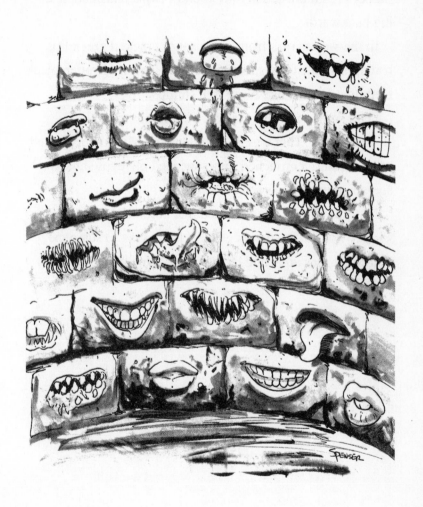

creaking of an old rocking ch—

Eh-heh-heh-heh-heh!

A blood-curdling witch's cackle cut my thought short. Stinky breath blasted my neck, and I twisted around, leaping backward.

In the wall across from me, a set of cracked green lips had appeared. They smiled hideously, showing rotten black teeth that looked like burnt tree stumps.

"Did someone call for a witch?" the lips rasped.

That did it. That was all I could take. My bravery lasted only so long. I crouched low, squeezed my eyes shut, and screamed until I was out of breath.

Ninespire hadn't been turned into some cheesy old spooky house. Its ghouls weren't just trying to scare me. Ninespire was alive and trying to drive me totally insane.

5

More mouths appeared as I screamed. Slobbering, spitting mouths, and mouths with tongues as long as my arms. They babbled, laughed, and greedily licked the walls like kids slurping syrup from their chins.

When I couldn't scream anymore, they took over. The moan stones screeched and shrieked until my skin crawled. Then they started to speak.

One voice reminded me of a lost child begging for her mother. Another sounded like a frightened animal caught in a trap.

Those were the ones I could bear to think about. The others were more horrible. They belonged to the angry beasts that lurked in nightmares.

"Chomp her bones!" one howled, smacking its flabby lips.

"Slurp up her hair like spaghetti!" another whined so

pitifully that I could almost feel its hunger.

"Gnaw on her toenails!"

The awful screeches went on and on. I pressed my hands to my ears, but it didn't help. Not even my own screams could block the voices out.

So I finally did the only thing I could do. I got angry. I jumped up, balled my hands into fists, threw back my head, and roared.

"SHUT UP!"

I can be loud when I want to be. Really loud. And just then I wanted to make more noise than an ogre singing in the bathtub.

I screamed until I thought my eyeballs would pop out, louder than the loudest moan stone. When I snapped my mouth shut, I heard nothing but sweet, undisturbed silence. The moan stones had gotten the hint.

"There now," I panted, rotating to stare at the dozens of mouths on the walls. "That's better."

Most of the mouths had closed. A few had even disap-peared. But one decided to test its luck.

"Boo!" it teased in a velvety purr. Then it puckered its lips and blew me a sloppy kiss.

There's a clown in every class, I told myself. Then I closed my eyes and forced myself to count slowly to ten. I wasn't afraid anymore. I was bordering on furious.

The sassy mouth snickered smugly. "Looks like I showed h—" it started to boast.

I didn't let it finish.

As fast as a lady knight draws her sword, I snatched the oilcan that hung on my tool belt, aimed, and fired. Three fast squeezes sent slippery blasts of oil streaming toward my target.

Splurk! Splurk! Splurk!

Bull's-eye! Oil streaked straight into the sassy mouth, splashing its rubbery tongue and lips.

"*Glach!*" the mouth spat, scrunching up in a sorry look. "What's the ... *bleh!* ... big idea?"

Now it was my turn to snicker, but I was careful to keep my oilcan raised.

"There's more where that came from," I promised. "Now be a nice slobbery mouth and show me the way out of here." I had to make fast use of my advantage.

The mouth continued to pucker. "I can't!" it grumbled. "Do ... *yech!* ... I look like I have arms to you?"

I rolled my eyes and shook the oilcan threateningly.

"All right, *tell* me how to get out," I demanded.

The mouth groaned instead of answering. "I think I'm going to be sick."

I crossed my eyes. "The way out? Or do you want some more?" I pressed.

"Oh, fine, fine! Look up! Don't let my discomfort concern you." The mouth really knew how to put on a show, but I wasn't going to feel sorry for it.

High overhead was a trapdoor in the ceiling. At least

twenty unpleasant-looking mouths separated me from it. The door was a long way up and suspiciously pink.

"And just how am I supposed to get up there?" I asked, not really expecting help from the moan stones. What I got surprised me.

Pppbbbttt!

A mouth to my right stuck out its gooey tongue and let loose a noisy raspberry. I gave a start and then spun to face it, raising my oilcan.

"Another wise g—" I started, but a chorus of wet raspberries burst out all over the room, cutting me off.

Pppbbbttt! Pppbbbttt!

Every moan stone mouth joined the slobbery fun. Pink tongues, green tongues, and even a polka-dotted tongue sloppily sprayed the walls with slime.

I sucked in a deep breath, preparing to scream again.

"The way out, Princess Oilcan," the sassy mouth announced, interrupting my scream.

The raspberries had stopped, but the tongues remained sticking out of the mouths. They didn't move and were as stiff as planks thrust over the sides of pirate ships. They almost reminded me of—

Stairs.

The tongues were spaced evenly along the walls, and I followed them with my eyes from bottom to top. Sure enough, they formed a sort of circular stairway that led to the trapdoor in the ceiling.

I was supposed to climb a stairway of slobbery tongues.

"Huwwy, Pwintheth Oh-ulcan," requested a mouth with two fat lips. It didn't pull in its tongue, so it spoke with an exaggerated lisp. "We don' haff awl day."

I shrugged and reattached the oilcan to my belt. Then I stepped onto the lowest tongue and started to climb.

Tongue Tide

6

I tried hard not to think about what I was doing. I tried, but I couldn't help myself.

I was climbing a stairway made out of tongues! Years later I would still think about it with a shudder. Double yuck!

Sklurk! Glook! Splick!

The tongues squished beneath my feet as if I were stepping on stacks of moist pillows. They quivered and drooled but held themselves rigid until I passed.

Then the comments and jokes started. As soon as I stepped from one tongue to the next, the lower tongue began mouthing off.

"Pee-yew! When was the last time you changed your socks?"

"That's putting your foot in my mouth!"

"What are your boots made of—dead fish?"

The remarks only got worse from there. The moan stones, it seemed, were as good at insulting as they were at moaning.

I finally made it to the top of the stairs and took a closer look at the pink trapdoor. Just as I'd suspected, it was another tongue. I was going to have to touch this one with my hands.

Thankfully I kept a pair of work gloves tucked into my belt. I didn't mind a little dirt—*no grime, no crime*, I liked to say—but a tinker needs to be prepared for the extra messy jobs. There are some things that even I didn't want to touch.

Again I tried not to think about what I was doing. First I pushed with my hands, then my arms, and finally my shoulders. The tongue-door budged slowly, oozing open with a sickening slurp.

Sklur-r-rrpp!

Strands of sticky goo splattered the walls and me. I shuddered in disgust and squeezed quickly through the opening. As I went, the tongue oozed across my back like a lick from an over-friendly whale.

The experience gave a whole new meaning to *no grime, no crime*. In this case, *slime* was the crime. Triple yuck!

The trapdoor led to a familiar room, and I sighed with relief when I saw it. I'd had enough of frogs, tongues, and moan stones. I was supposed to be making a Gidget-gadget delivery, not having a slime-filled adventure.

Then my eyes did a double-take. My adventure wasn't over yet.

The room was the usual entryway to Ninespire. But today there was one difference. A *big* difference.

The room and everything in it were huge. A giant staircase with steps as tall as me curved up to an archway above. Framed paintings the size of barn doors hung on the walls. I felt as if I'd climbed to the top of a magic beanstalk.

I glanced at my hands and wiggled my fingers. They *looked* normal-sized. I shouted, "Hello, hello!" Except for a lonely echo, my voiced sounded normal, too, not squeaky small.

What was going on here? Had I shrunk or had the room grown?

V-v-vwerrrrr!

A pile of oversized metal parts, gears, and gadgets in the center of the room began to twitch and then spin. Gadgets screeched and clanked deafeningly.

"*M*-Mephello?" I stammered, rapidly backing away.

The pile was actually a mechanical man called a golem. My father had built him for Wizard Ast, with my help, of course.

The golem's name was Mephello, and it was his job to greet visitors to Ninespire. When he wasn't working, Mephello lay down in a heap on the floor. That was his way of resting.

V-V-VWERRRRR!

Mephello continued spinning and started to float up off the floor. His gears slid and clicked together, taking shape. Soon he resembled a giant metal skeleton, not a pile of mixed-up gadgets.

By giant, I meant *gigantic*. The last time I had seen him, Mephello had been ten feet tall. That's how big my father and I had built him. Today Mephello was as tall as a two-story building.

"Stop, Mephello!" I barked firmly. On a normal day, the golem would recognize my voice and obey. But today was anything but normal.

DROOM!

Mephello's iron feet slammed onto the floor. To me, they were the size of canoes. His eyes burned like torches as he stared down from far, far above.

"*Whiz-click,*" he buzzed so loudly that the gadgets in my backpack rattled. "*In*-intruder!"

I shrieked and started to run. Mephello wasn't the nice, helpful golem I'd helped build. He was a monstrous iron skeleton that had decided I was an enemy.

Scoot Boots

7

I sprinted for the stairs. The trapdoor led to the moan stones and a dead end. There was no door in that tower, so I couldn't go back the way I had come. The stairs were my only hope.

Droom! Droom! The golem gave chase, his massive feet pounding on the floor. He was close—too close—but I didn't turn or look back. Hearing him was enough.

Just before I reached the overgrown stairs, I jumped. They were too tall to climb, and I needed a secret weapon to make it up them.

In mid-leap, I raised my knees, reached down, and slapped the hidden buttons built into the sides of my boots.

A pair of clunky boots wasn't usually the most comfort-able thing to wear, but mine were special. I called them *scoot boots*, and they were spring-loaded. When I pressed their buttons, springs popped from the bottoms of their soles.

Sploing!

I hit the floor in front of the first stair and bounced. Soaring high, I pumped my arms as if I were running a race. My momentum carried me onto the step above.

Sploing! When I hit it, I bounced again.

"Gidget and her gadgets ride again!" I whooped, thrilled with pride. I was almost flying because of a gadget I had built with my own hands. What a great feeling!

"Intru-*tru*-der!" Mephello bellowed in a mechanical stutter, refusing to give up. His gears whirred and screeched. I wasn't out of trouble yet.

Sploing! Sploing! I kept bouncing. *Droom! Droom!* Mephello kept chasing.

Up the stairs we went, making quite a racket. If Wizard Ast hadn't known he had a visitor, our noise surely told him that something strange was going on.

I reached the archway at the top of the stairs a heartbeat ahead of Mephello. My scoot boots propelled me into the air one last time and—

Kloomp!

—sent me crashing into the ceiling.

"Ooof!" I grunted, dropping sharply to the floor.

That was something I hadn't counted on—a low ceiling. The room behind me was gigantic, but the hallway beyond the arch was normal-sized. There was no room for bouncing.

"*I-i*-intruder!" Mephello roared again, almost to the top of the stairs.

I threw myself backward, half-scampering and half-sliding on my backside. Mephello filled the archway and reached into the hall.

Sclamp! Sclamp! His hands snapped like lobsterpod claws trying to snatch me.

I sucked in a breath, preparing to scream. I had only so many gadgets that could save me in emergencies.

Sclamp! Mephello's hands snapped again. His arms stretched. His fingers reached. But the rest of him came no closer.

I was saved!

"You're too big to fit in here!" I shouted. "Neener, neener, neener!" I was so excited that I actually stuck my thumbs in my ears and flapped my hands back and forth.

It was a silly gesture, but I was elated. Mephello was too big to fit into the normal-sized hall. Luck had rescued me from another one of Ninespire's unusual traps.

The hall beyond the archway didn't look familiar. It was empty and turned to the left a short distance ahead.

After a moment of thought, I shrugged and started walking. Where else was I supposed to go?

"Do *n*-not go *th-th*-that way, intruder," Mephello warned threateningly. His voice screeched like rusty bolts being turned too tightly.

I ignored him and walked faster. *Nothing can be worse*

36

than moan stones and a crazy, overgrown golem, I thought, trying to reassure myself.

But when I turned the corner, I found out just how wrong I was.

Look Who's Talking

8

Www-a-a-a-a-ahhh!

A piercing cry cut through the hall, forcing me to cover my ears. It was a cry of hunger and a cry of unhappiness. It was the cry of a crabby three-year-old.

I had heard similar cries plenty of times before. My little brother used to shriek the same way. He was older now, so he saved his tantrums for when they counted most, but I would never forget the sound.

"Wizard Ast?" I called hopefully. No, I didn't think the wizard was crying, but he could have a visitor.

Www-a-a-a-a-ahhh! The baby's wail drowned out the sound of my voice. I was going to have to investigate.

The hallway wound around impossibly, like a ball of string. At its end stood a brightly-painted blue door stenciled with silver stars.

I recognized the door immediately, and couldn't keep

from smiling. It was the door to Simon's room. Simon, Wizard Ast's red-haired apprentice, was a boy my age and my friend.

"Finally," I sighed, reaching for the handle. At last I would see a familiar face in the mixed-up, goofy castle.

I threw open the door, jumped inside, and shouted, "Hi, Simon!" My good feeling lasted until my feet hit the floor.

Www-a-a-a-a-ahhh!

The baby's screech stung my ears more than ever. It was immediately followed by a scolding accusation.

"You scared him!"

A girl sat cross-legged on Simon's bed, cradling a red-haired toddler in her arms. The girl looked familiar, but I hadn't seen her in a while, and never in such wild clothes.

She had shoulder-length auburn hair, not quite brown and not quite red. She wore a green tunic with one blue sleeve and one yellow, purple slacks, golden slippers, and a floppy, belled cap.

After a moment's thought, I decided that the girl had to be Simon's sister. The room was just the way I remembered it, except for three new doors on one wall. They'd never been there before.

The doors were made of black metal and shaped like beakers used in science experiments. Their hollow handles were made of clear glass, and colorful liquid bubbled inside them.

"AnnaBell?" I asked the girl doubtfully.

"Oh, Gidget!" she sobbed almost as loudly as the baby. "What's happening?"

Her voice gave her away. The girl was AnnaBell, Simon's little sister. She was a couple of years younger than I was.

"There was an explosion," I answered quickly, scanning the room. "Where's Simon? We need him." Simon understood magic and would be able to explain the weird things that were happening.

Surprisingly, it wasn't AnnaBell who spoke next. The toddler in her arms stopped crying, sniffled, and peered at me.

"Me Simo," he said seriously. "Gidgi come to save day?"

My mouth fell open in dismay. Things couldn't get any worse. My friend Simon had been turned into a baby!

Goblin Delight

9

"Simon!" I cried. "What happened?"

The toddler in AnnaBell's arms shook his little head meaningfully. "Not me," he declared.

I blinked again, glancing at AnnaBell. "What? Why won't he help us?" I sputtered.

AnnaBell frowned and drew Simon in close, tenderly propping his chin on her shoulder. "He's only three, Gidget. What do you want from him?"

"But …!" I tossed my arms up helplessly. Arguing was pointless. Simon really was three years old. He wouldn't respond to yelling or demands.

"Who's going to help us now?" I muttered, feeling sorry for myself. Finding Simon and his sister hadn't made anything better.

Simon heard me and reached out to pat my cheek. His tiny hand felt warm and reassuring.

"There still you, Gidgi," he told me hopefully.

I squinted at him, confused. His toddler-talk had me stumped. What was he trying to say?

"It's one of *The Noble Deeds and Duties*," AnnaBell explained. "Act Thirty-seven, I think. *When There Is No One Else, There Is Still You.*"

The Noble Deeds and Duties was a code of behavior for knights and heroes. One hundred different Acts made up the code. Simon knew them all backward and frontward.

He also knew who could save us from Castle Ninespire and its dangers. We could. Until we found Wizard Ast, we had to be our own heroes.

"Have you opened any of these doors?" I asked, meaning the large black ones shaped like beakers. If we had to be heroes, I figured we might as well get started.

AnnaBell shook her head, causing the bells on her cap to jingle. "Not yet. Why don't we go back the way you came in?"

She was afraid, I realized, and I couldn't blame her. She didn't want to investigate Ninespire or find Wizard Ast. She wanted to escape.

"I'll open the first one," I offered. I decided not to tell her about Mephello or the moan stones. "And I promise not to get myself turned into a baby."

I started toward the door, but AnnaBell snorted loudly, so I stopped short.

"A baby," she said sarcastically. "Good one. That was so

funny I forgot to laugh."

Her words were a challenge if I'd ever heard one. "Think you can do better?" I challenged right back.

Instead of answering, AnnaBell asked her own question. "What did the goblin do after he swallowed a firefly?"

"What in the world … oh, I get it," I bumbled, slow to catch on. Her question was a joke. "I don't know. What did the goblin do after he swallowed a firefly?"

AnnaBell paused for effect. "He burped with de-*light!*" she giggled. "Bah-bah-boom!"

I held a straight face for as long as I could, then I burst into giggles, too. The joke wasn't that funny, but her timing had been perfect. We'd needed some silliness.

"Firefly … de-light," I snickered. "Very clever."

AnnaBell beamed proudly. "I know! I'm practicing to be a jester."

So that's it, I realized. AnnaBell was dressed like a jester to make people laugh. Her colorful outfit was a costume and part of her act.

"Here," she said, standing up and handing Simon to me. "I'll open the first door."

Simon stared at me intensely. "Pig-back," he ordered.

When my brother had been younger, Mom told me that babies ruled the house. She called them little kings and queens. Hearing Simon now, I knew that she'd been right. He wanted a piggyback ride, and he wouldn't take no for an answer.

So I tucked King Simon into my backpack. Just his head, shoulders, and arms stuck out. Then I buttoned up the rest of him snugly so that he couldn't fall or escape.

There you go, Your Majesty, I snickered to myself. *Enjoy your new throne.* The little king had his wish, and I had him safely out of the way.

"Hold on to your hat," AnnaBell advised, reaching for the nearest door handle.

She wasn't so afraid anymore, I realized. Telling a joke must have gotten her mind off danger.

Blur-bur-bur-bur-bur-burp, bur-r-r.

Instead of creaking, the beaker-shaped door made a kind of bubbly burp as it opened. Then AnnaBell shrieked and slammed it shut immediately.

She rounded on me, her eyes wide with terror.

"Not that way!" she gasped. "There are *monsters* in there!"

10

"What did you see? I asked AnnaBell breathlessly.

AnnaBell was staring at me with unblinking eyes. Her lips moved but didn't make a sound.

"Trust me," she finally replied. "You *don't* want to go in there."

I bit my bottom lip to keep from disagreeing. One little peek into the room couldn't hurt. I was dying to see!

"Please," AnnaBell begged. In my backpack, Simon detected her fear and started to cry again.

Www-a-a-a-ahhh!

"All right, all right!" I relented. "I'll try a different door."

Simon snapped his mouth shut, his eyes instantly dry. He might have been only three, but he knew how to get what he wanted. The little king!

To my astonishment, the door AnnaBell had opened was

gone. Not closed. *Gone*. Solid wall stood where it had been.

"*Rusty buckets!*" I swore under my breath. Did Ninespire's madness ever take a break?

Trying not to think about the missing door, I cracked open the second and peeked inside. It belched slowly, same as the first.

Blur-bur-bur-bur-bur-burp, bur-r-r-r.

Beyond was a room cluttered with ruined equipment. Shattered glass and cracked beakers twinkled on the floor. Wooden workbenches and racks that looked as if they had been half-eaten lay on their sides or upside down.

What eats furniture? I asked myself. But aloud, I reported, "Something happened in here. There's broken glass—"

Blam!

AnnaBell kicked the door, banging it shut and almost taking off my nose.

"Get back!" she howled, her face turning pale.

I flinched backward, covering my nose. "What did you see this time?"

AnnaBell's face was ghostly white. "I don't know how, Gidget, but both doors lead to the same spot in the same room." Her eyes narrowed and she glanced suspiciously at the third door. "And I'll bet that one does, too."

My eyes darted to the third door, and I nodded. In mixed-up Ninespire, finding three doors that led to the exact same

46

place wouldn't surprise me. Not after what I'd seen.

"We have to open it," I told her softly. "There's no other way out."

It was a fact. The second door had disappeared along with the first. The third was our only choice.

This time I didn't give AnnaBell the chance to interfere or almost take off my nose. I flung the door open as if I expected to find treasure on the other side.

Blur, bur-bur-bur-bur-burp, bur-r-r.

Just as I'd thought, I saw the messy room again. But this time I didn't gawk at the broken glass and chewed-up furniture. The monsters had my full attention.

"I told you!" AnnaBell screeched, pointing frantically at the ceiling.

Glurga-bluh-bloop! Glurga-bloop!

Dozens of foamy creatures floated in the air like jellyfish in the sea. They were shaped like clumps of lint found under an old sofa, and were the size of housecats. Their bubbly bodies reminded me of dirty, sudsy dishwater—ugh!

That was it! *Ugsuds!* That was what I would call them.

"Ugsuds, that's perfect!" AnnaBell agreed. I hadn't even realized that I'd said the made-up name out loud.

From the doorway, we watched the ugsuds gurgle and glide around the room. They snatched furniture and tools with their long, gooey tentacles and jammed them into their foamy mouths.

Whatever went in those mouths never came out. It

47

vanished and was swallowed with a loud ugsud burp.
Glurga-bloop!

That explains the chewed-up look, I thought darkly. The
ugsuds were gobbling up the room one acidy bite at a time.

"Don't let them bite you!" I shouted above the nonstop
belching. The ugsuds could devour metal and wood.
Imagine what they could do to us!

AnnaBell didn't hesitate. "Watch me pull a rabbit out of
my hat," she said. Then she reached into her sleeve and
pulled out a deck of playing cards. "Bah-bah-boom!"

I glanced at her with concern. Did she think the ugsuds
wanted to play a hand of *Go Fish*?

"What are you doing?" I bellowed. "Card tricks won't
save us!"

AnnaBell winked at me and then bounded into the room.
Spinning and rolling, she leaped from shelf to workbench to
overturned chair. Her small body was a colorful blur of
speed.

Seeing her bravery, I didn't hesitate either. I charged
after her with a yell. If my friend was going to die, I
wouldn't let her do it alone.

Card Tricks

11

"AnnaBell, slow down!" I cried, using my extra-loud voice.

She was still bounding around the room. Her small feet skimmed furniture as she expertly leaped from one half-eaten piece to the next.

"Wait up!"

AnnaBell didn't slow. She twirled and rolled and shuffled her deck of cards on the fly. Then she attacked the ugsuds as gracefully as a dancer in a ballet.

"Seven spades be slashing blades!" she cried, flicking her wrist.

A single card streaked from her fingertips, cutting through the air as sure as an arrow. It struck the bubble-body of the nearest ugsud, and the monster popped like a stuck balloon.

Sploop!

Sticky wetness spattered us like the spray from a shaken paintbrush. Gross, but the ugsud was gone.

"Good shot!" I cheered, slapping down my goggles. See how often they came in handy?

But the ugsuds weren't impressed with my goggles, and they didn't give us time to celebrate. They belched angrily and attacked.

Glurga-bloop! Glurga-bloop!

A cluster of foamy blobs zipped at my head, forcing me to dive to the floor. Sloppy mouths smacked and slurped. Tentacles drooled slime into my hair.

I rolled to my knees and whipped out my slingshot. It was time for a little target practice.

In one of my belt's pockets, I stored nuts and bolts. They were tinkering supplies, but would work as ammo. I loaded one into my slingshot, drew back, took aim at the nearest ugsud, and fired.

Thwipp! Sploop!

My first shot scored a direct hit. It pierced the approaching ugsud's bulbous body, and the little brute exploded. Thick liquid splattered across the floor in clumps like spoonfuls of spilled pudding.

One down and three hundred to go, I thought grimly.

I didn't have enough nuts and bolts to splatter them all, but I promised myself that I'd put up a good fight. My hands and arms blurred as I loaded and fired.

Thwipp! Sploop! Thwipp! Sploop!

AnnaBell leaped lightly to my side. Her eyes sparkled mischievously, and her small face was flushed with excitement.

"To your right—duck!" she shouted, spinning on her toes. The musical jingle of her jester's cap seemed out of place.

I obeyed without question and threw myself low. Something wet slid across the back of my neck, but I felt no pain. What a close one!

"Thanks!" I panted, scrambling back to my knees.

AnnaBell grunted and snapped her wrist forward. "Red queen take heart, sting like a dart!" she cried, launching another card.

Her aim was as good as mine was. *Sploop!* The ugsud that had slimed my neck exploded.

"Welcome!" she added breathlessly. Then she bent her knees and leaned back so far that her hair almost touched the floor.

"How—?" I started, but AnnaBell's voice drowned mine out.

"Black deuce is wild! Ugsuds be mild!" Before dropping onto her back, she whipped a card from each hand straight up into the air.

Sploop! Sploop! Overhead, two more ugsuds popped harmlessly.

There was more to being a jester than jokes and silly costumes, I realized. AnnaBell was fierce and fast. Maybe she had learned a few magical secrets from her brother, too.

But Simon wasn't as excited about his sister's bravery as I was. He thrashed in my backpack for all he was worth, trying to squirm free.

"Bad poshuns!" he shrieked over and over.

His words almost stopped me dead in my tracks. He was yelling at the ugsuds, calling them *potions*.

Suddenly everything about the unusual room made sense. The beaker-shaped doors, the broken glass, the bubbly ugsuds. They were clues that hinted at what this room was used for.

We were in Wizard Ast's magic potion laboratory. The blobs we were fighting weren't real monsters. They were potions that had come to life and gone crazy.

No reason to be surprised, I told myself. Just about everything else in Castle Ninespire had gone mad. Why not a laboratory full of magic potions?

"Bad, bad!" Simon screeched. "Lemme down, Gidgi! Lemme down!" He kicked his heels into my back, ruining my shot at an ugsud.

Thwipp! Flooo! It was a clean miss.

I looked to AnnaBell for help. I couldn't aim with Simon kicking and screaming, and the ugsuds were swarming closer.

"What am I supposed to do?" I pleaded. There wasn't any time to calm baby King Simon.

AnnaBell glanced at me and her eyes went wide. "Be careful, Gidget! He's trying to cast a spell!"

My eyes widened farther than hers had. Simon was only three-years-old. His magic would probably hurt us more than the ugsuds.

A Hero's Heart

12

"Make him stop!" I bellowed at AnnaBell. "You're his sister—do something!"

Simon was still getting ready to cast a spell. He couldn't even pronounce the letter *R*, but he thought he was big enough for magic. Ridiculous!

AnnaBell shrugged helplessly. It was too late to stop her brother. He was trying to help in his three-year-old's way.

AnnaBell shot me an apologetic look, then spun quickly to her left. She let loose a flurry of cards, shouting, "My royal flush strikes in a rush!"

Sploop! Sploop! Sploop-sploop! Sploop!

Five cards hit five different ugsuds. The brutes popped, but more glided toward us. There never seemed to be fewer of them.

Luckily, Simon came to our rescue.

He suddenly stopped kicking and became very still. Then

his tiny voice squeaked shrilly in my ears.

Gwow big, bubbles! Swell! Expand!
Be wike hippos! Buwst wais'bands!

When he stopped speaking, the ugsuds started to grow.

All around the laboratory, the brutes swelled larger and larger. Their bodies grew from the size of cats to dogs to ponies in seconds. Soon they would be big enough to swallow us whole.

What have you done? I wanted to shriek.

Simon cheered. "Hooway, hooway!" I could even feel his stubby little arms pumping in triumph. "Lookee-look!"

I spun in a half-circle and came face to foam with a bloated ugsud. The thing quivered inches away, its mouth drooling madly. Its body bubbled bigger one last time then exploded.

SPLORP!

Liquid drenched my face and hair, and I sucked in a breath to scream. Ninespire hadn't just gone crazy, it had gone disgusting. First slobbery tongues, now exploding ugsuds. I had a lot to scream about. Quadruple yuck!

But the ugsuds spoiled my chance. One by one, all of them exploded.

SPLORP! SPLORP! Foamy fluid splattered the walls.
SPLORP! SPLORP! Slime splashed every which way.

Seeing that, I realized that Simon's spell was helping us.

His magic was making the ugsuds grow and grow until they burst. We were saved!

"Hooray, Simon!" I cheered.

"Under here!" AnnaBell beckoned, diving beneath a three-legged table. I scurried after her as fast as I could. Simon clapped his pudgy hands merrily.

"I did it!" he squealed.

"You sure did, Simon," AnnaBell smiled breathlessly. *"The Heart of a Hero Is Not Measured By Size."*

Her words, I knew, were another Act from *The Noble Deeds and Duties*. They meant that it didn't matter how big or old a person was, everyone could do good and help others.

"Yay!" Simon beamed, sounding so proud of himself.

For the next several minutes, we huddled quietly under the table. The exploding ugsuds made plenty of noise without us. Simon had seen to that.

S-s-s-s-PLORP!

The last ugsud hissed like a leaky balloon before exploding. I wasn't sorry to hear it go.

"Now let's get out of here," AnnaBell said quickly, her eyes staring urgently into mine.

I quickly looked away. She had behaved so bravely during our battle. I hated to disappoint her now. I hated to tell her what I'd seen earlier.

Ninespire was up to its crazy tricks again. The third beaker-shaped door was gone. It had vanished along with the other two.

"There isn't a door," I whispered. "We're stuck here."

13

"There has to be a way out!" AnnaBell cried. Wild-eyed, she scrambled from under the table. "Maybe there's a secret door."

I followed her out into the center of the foam-covered floor and started to pace. If I had ever needed to think my best, it was then. We were trapped in a wizard's laboratory without doors.

Right away, I remembered that I'd been in a similar situation recently. The moan stones' tower hadn't had a door at first either. Not until I'd looked closer, that is.

Maybe all of the weirdness in Ninespire was like that. Maybe it could be figured out. After all, even the ugsuds had had a weakness.

AnnaBell was frantically peeking under furniture. She moved quickly but clumsily, and that told me she was afraid. The thought of being trapped scared her.

It scared me, too, but I knew Ninespire's secret now. AnnaBell didn't. The room had a way out. We just had to find it.

Still pacing, I carefully scanned the room. A hidden door could be anywhere.

Ugsud-chomped shelves stood against the walls. Over-turned tables and benches hid much of the floor. The only thing that resembled a door was too tiny to take seriously.

It was a mouse hole in a corner.

I tried to ignore the hole and keep pacing but couldn't. My eyes kept looking back. Every time they did, the same thought popped into my head.

That hole has to go somewhere.

Finally I threw up my arms and let out a big sigh. I knew when I was beaten.

"There," I pointed at the mouse hole. "That's how we get out."

AnnaBell snorted doubtfully. "Did an ugsud hit you on the head? We can't fit in there. Let *me* make the jokes from now on."

This was the part of my plan that I really didn't like. We couldn't *normally* fit into the mouse hole. But we could *magically* fit. That meant Simon.

I closed my eyes when I spoke next. "Simon, can you make us small? We have to get into that mouse house."

"Wheee!" Simon hooted as if I'd given him dessert before dinner.

AnnaBell wasn't so happy. She gasped and stared at me with her mouth open. I'm pretty sure she was too surprised to speak. But I didn't need her to tell me that I was asking for trouble.

Simon was only three and had already used his magic without blowing us up. What were the chances of it working safely again?

He'll probably make me the size of a house, not a mouse, I worried silently. *Rusty buckets, what am I getting us into?*

Before I could open my mouth to call the whole thing off, Simon started to chant.

Big, small, little, tall.
Wide, fin, nawwow, spwawl.

Size change, altered—strange!
Mouse hole, rodent range.

He finished and AnnaBell exhaled loudly.

"Nothing happened," she said, sounding relieved. "Now let's find the real doo—"

"Lemme down," Simon interrupted. "Huwwy!"

I obeyed immediately. Unlike AnnaBell, I didn't think Simon's spell would do nothing. Something was going to happen.

And if we didn't follow Simon's rules, that something would be bad.

After he was out of my backpack, Simon pulled two

unusual flowers from a pocket.

"Smell," he ordered, holding one flower to AnnaBell and one to me. The two of us glanced at each other, then did as King Simon commanded.

Aaah-choo! I sneezed.

Aaah-choo! AnnaBell echoed.

The flowers had pink and blue petals that looked like pillows. They also gave off a strong vanilla scent. We couldn't keep from sneezing.

"Yum!" AnnaBell exclaimed. "Where'd you … ?" Her question died as she let out a strangled sound. "Simon, you're huge!"

I opened my eyes, surprised to find that I'd had them closed. The furniture in the room looked as if it belonged to a giant. Three-year-old Simon towered over me the way Mephello had.

"You did it!" I cheered at him. "We're tiny. But what about you?"

"My tuwn!" Simon giggled, his voice sounding terrifyingly big and far away. Then in a very grown-up way, he pushed up his sleeves and spoke in a slow voice.

A mouse's house is fine by me.
I'll seize some cheese and wun home fwee.

Oh, no! I gasped silently. *Not another spell!* Twice was dangerous enough. Three times was begging for trouble.

Dark smoke poured from the sleeves of Simon's robe. It

smelled of cheddar cheese and quickly surrounded him. He coughed once, then vanished.

14

Simon was gone. The smoke thickened. It churned rapidly and rushed toward the floor as if being sucked into a hose.

"*It*-it's changing," AnnaBell hissed, clutching my sleeve.

Huddling close, we watched the impossible. The smoke sank instead of rising. It clumped together instead of drifting apart.

This is bad, I told myself again, and not for the last time. Simon's latest spell was going as crazy as Castle Ninespire.

The smoke slowly changed color from black to grey to white. Then it formed a solid, four-legged shape and wasn't smoke anymore. The overwhelming smell of cheddar cheese returned, almost making me gag.

"*Squeak,*" said a mouse that hadn't been there a moment before.

AnnaBell and I jumped back, our mouths dropping open.

The mouse was as big as we were.

"Stay back," I warned the mouse, taking a cautious step backward. Slowly I reached for my slingshot.

"*Squeak*-stop!" the mouse chirped in a familiar voice. "It's me!"

I froze with my hand hovering over my slingshot. Something funny was going on. The mouse had sounded exactly like—

"*Simon!*" AnnaBell and I cried at the same time.

Suddenly I felt foolish. Simon's spell hadn't gone crazy. It had turned him into a mouse. He was now the perfect size and shape to escape into the mouse hole. What a great spell!

"*Squeak*-sit on my back," Simon the mouse offered, crouching low.

AnnaBell whooped with delight. "I get to be your first flea!" she squealed. Then she hugged her furry brother around the neck before climbing onto his back.

I patted mouse-Simon's nose and then took an uneasy seat behind AnnaBell. Riding a mouse had sounded like a good idea, but actually doing it was weird.

Imagining AnnaBell biting Simon like a flea didn't help either.

After we were seated and clutching clumps of his fur, Simon scampered for the mouse hole. As usual, AnnaBell couldn't keep from chattering.

"Why did the mouse cross the laboratory?" she blurted.

Hearing such an old joke made me sigh. AnnaBell had changed a few words, but everyone had heard the one about the chicken crossing the road.

"To get to the other side," I said, trying not to sound too bored.

AnnaBell frowned for a moment before trying again. "Why did the *lion* cross the laboratory?"

I shrugged, not interested repeating the old punch line. "I don't know."

"To get to the other *pride!*" AnnaBell snickered. "Pride, get it? Lions gather in groups called prides. Bah-bah-boom! Now what about the fish?"

I shrugged again. I'd gotten the joke. It just hadn't been funny.

"To get to the other *tide*," she continued. "And the flower girl?"

This time I crossed my eyes at her.

"To get to the other—" AnnaBell started.

"—bride!" I finished, barking a laugh I couldn't hold back. AnnaBell's jokes really weren't very funny, but she tried hard telling them.

Still chuckling, we sped through the mouse hole. The light dimmed and the walls closed in. It felt as if we had slipped into a long-forgotten secret passage.

Our laughter faded rapidly, too. The passageway wasn't the cozy mouse-house we'd expected. There was no soft bed made of shredded paper. There were no delicious chunks of tender orange cheese.

The mouse hole led to a filthy maze of tunnels filled with cobwebs and worse. I doubted that we were better off in them than in the laboratory. At least the lab hadn't smelled so ... so *mousy*.

Simon, of course, didn't seem to mind the smell. He probably didn't even notice, being a mouse himself.

He darted down tunnel after tunnel, pausing to sniff at every fork in our path. Then he would pick a direction and waddle into a run, saying, "I'm *squeak*-sure the food is this way."

After hearing that for about the third time, AnnaBell winked at me. "Boys always think about food," she said just loud enough for her brother to hear.

Simon bucked once like a wild bronco but didn't squeak a word.

We finally came to a second mouse hole. Light shone through from its other side, and the sweet scents of fresh bread and ripe fruit filled the air.

That's probably the dinner Wizard Ast was making for me, I told myself glumly. After all I'd been through, I'd earned a double helping of kingbite cookies for dessert.

"The kitchen!" AnnaBell groaned at her brother. "You found the kitchen instead of Wizard Ast? Instead of the front door?"

Simon ignored her, his nose and whiskers twitching busily. "There's trouble out there," he told us. "I *squeak-*

smell it."

"Rusty buckets, what kind of trouble?" I muttered. We had already been shrunk to the size of eggs and were sitting on the back of a mouse. Wasn't that trouble enough?

Simon shivered and flattened his ears against his head.

"*C*-cats," he whispered. "Wizard Ast's cats are *squeak*-somewhere in the kitchen."

AnnaBell groaned again, understanding the danger. We were only three inches tall. The wizard's cats would enjoy chasing down a mouse and two mouse-sized girls. What they would do after that was anybody's guess, but I had a few ideas.

"We might as well be carrying catnip in our pockets," AnnaBell grumbled hopelessly.

Dancing Bananas

15

"Maybe the cats are asleep," I suggested.

Even before the words left my mouth, I didn't believe them. Ninespire had gone crazy and had taken our luck with it. That meant Wizard Ast's cats would be hungry and on the prowl.

AnnaBell leaned down to wiggle her fingers in front of Simon's fuzzy face. "Why not use magic?" she asked. "Turn yourself into a dog."

What a great idea! Although cats and dogs get along better than many people think, Simon the dog would be safer than Simon the delicious-looking mouse.

"Be a baron mastiff," I said, naming the biggest kind of dog I knew.

To my disappointment, Simon sighed. "I can't," he admitted. "I can't use magic when I'm in an animal's shape. No wizard can. I'm *squeak*-stuck."

The meaning of that hit me like a punch. "You can't even change back into a boy?"

Simon's whiskers wilted like thirsty flowers in the sun. "No. *Squeak*-someone else has to change me back. But at least I'm a grown-up mouse, not a baby one."

I blinked at that. He was right. Since turning himself into a mouse, Simon hadn't used baby talk or acted like a little king. He could even pronounce his R's now.

"Lucky me," AnnaBell chimed in. "Most big brothers grow up and get pimples. Mine turns himself into a rodent." She rolled her eyes dramatically.

The three of us laughed at that until a long, loud rumble came from beyond the mouse hole.

Purrrrrr-r-r-r!

The noise vibrated the walls inside the mouse hole, and clouds of dust swelled into the air. Whatever was causing the noise was close.

"Looks like your wish came true, Gidget," Simon whispered after the sound faded. "Hocus is *squeak*-sleeping."

I tilted my head thoughtfully. "You mean hocus pocus, right?" The two words went together. They were magic. No one said *abra* without *cadabra*. It was the same with hocus pocus.

"Uhh, not quite," Simon murmured unhelpfully. "Let me *squeak*-show you."

AnnaBell swiveled around, causing the bells on her cap to jingle. "Wait until you see this—and then don't!" Before she explained what that meant, Simon shuffled through the mouse hole and into the kitchen.

"What about the cats …?" I started. But the strange sights, smells, and happenings in the kitchen stunned me into silence. The room was a madhouse.

Boiling pots bubbled noisily, belching the melody to an old song. Pairs of peeled fruit twirled and danced on the countertops. Hard-boiled eggs played a dangerous game of follow-the-leader, some going so far as to roll off the tabletops.

Spleck! Spleck!

The odd sights would have horrified me anywhere else. But not in Ninespire. Not today. I expected them and had seen worse.

Dancing bananas indeed!

Before I could make a sound, AnnaBell clapped a hand over my mouth. With her other hand, she pointed at the biggest cat I'd ever seen.

It lay sprawled on its side, sleeping next to a small fireplace. Its chest rose and fell regularly, and its tail twitched as if the cat were enjoying a good dream.

Had I not been three inches tall, the cat would still have been huge. Its back was probably as high as an adult's thigh.

But the oddest thing about the animal was its coloring. Most of its body was as orange as a sunset. Its tail and ears, however, were inky black, inside and out.

As I gawked at it, the cat slowly peeked one eye open.

"Hocus," it purred. Then the claws on its paws sprang out.

16

"Everybody off" Simon squealed, bucking like a stallion again. "*Squeak*-spread out!"

AnnaBell and I half-jumped and half-slid from his back. She went right, and I went left. The cat pounced straight ahead.

Fw-w-watt!

A heavy paw came down on mouse-Simon's tail. He squealed again, stuck in place, and churned his legs uselessly. The cat had him pinned.

"Run!" he cried. "Hocus pocus!"

Running sounded like a great idea, but my feet wouldn't make up their mind. Simon needed help. I needed to escape. Which way should I go?

I hesitated and the cat decided for me.

One second it was there, a snarling orange giant of fur and fang. The next it was gone, and so was Simon. They vanished as suddenly as popped bubbles. There wasn't even time to scream.

Bloook!

That got my feet moving. Ninespire was up to its old tricks again, and I wasn't about to let any of them happen to me. I turned, sucked in a breath to scream, and—

Ran into a second cat as big as the first!

This cat was a mirror image of the first. It was mostly black but had an orange tail and ears. It was also huge.

"Pocus!" it snarled, swiping a paw at me.

I leaped just in time. Claws as thick as my fingers whisked past my face. If the cat hadn't snarled, its sneak attack would have found its mark.

Still, I stumbled awkwardly and tried to catch my balance. Nothing was making sense.

Had the cats really spoken? I'd only heard of one talking cat before, and that one had a silver ear.

"Look out below!" AnnaBell suddenly shouted.

Her words worried me almost as much as the cat did. She was almost out of playing cards. I couldn't imagine what she would try next.

Thur-deh-dur-dur!

I caught my balance and AnnaBell came tumbling in. It was either leap or be crushed.

"Beware the watermelon felon!" she howled.

Feet shuffling, she was riding a striped green watermelon as if it were a barrel or a log. It rumbled forward with her balanced on top of it.

Seeing her, I didn't know if I should laugh or scream. I'd heard of heroes riding to the rescue, but this was ridiculous. Heroes rode horses, not fruit!

Wheh-h-h-hhhhh!

Luckily, the wacky rescue confused the cat, too. It saw AnnaBell and the melon coming, hissed, and then turned tail and fled.

"Hocus pocus yourself!" I shouted after its lowered orange tail.

Bloook!

As soon as I said the words, the cat vanished, giving me an idea. There was something fishy going on, and it wasn't the smell of tuna on the cats' breath.

"Watch out!" AnnaBell huffed at me. "I can't exactly stop." She and the watermelon were almost on top of me.

"Oh, get down from there," I grumped. "The cat's gone."

AnnaBell shrugged and then hopped lightly to the floor. She was barely out of breath. The watermelon continued to roll without her.

Thinking about that, I shrugged. We were in a Ninespire gone mad. Watermelons were *supposed* to roll around by themselves.

"There's something weird about those cats," I told AnnaBell, forgetting the melon. "Whenever someone says *hocus pocus*, they disappear."

AnnaBell smiled at me. I'd seen her use the same smile

on three-year-old Simon.

"Well, sure," she agreed. "Everyone knows that. The cats are magic, and you can see only one of them at a time. Saying *hocus pocus* switches between them."

I put my hands on my hips. "You knew that already? Then why didn't you say it instead of goofing around on that melon?"

My friend grinned impishly. "My way was more fun. Besides, Hocus and Pocus wouldn't really hurt us. They're nice."

Hocus and Pocus. Finally something about the cats made sense. Hocus and Pocus were their names. That was what Simon had been trying to tell me. Hocus was the orange cat. Pocus was black.

Before AnnaBell could stop me, I yanked her jester's cap down over her eyes.

"Next time, do things the easy way!" I scolded her. "I was scared half to death!"

Kauch-th-hu!

I was ready to laugh, but something horrible and disgusting happened instead. The biggest, stickiest, messiest hairball I'd ever seen came slopping through the air.

Glack!

It slapped wetly against AnnaBell's back, knocking her to the floor. She threw her arms out, but the hairball was too heavy. It pinned her face-first to the floor like a spider's webbing. Quintuple yuck!

"Move!" she gasped. "I was wrong! The cats aren't nice anymore."

I knew immediately what had happened to Hocus and Pocus. Ninespire's madness had struck them, too.

Invisible to Visible

17

"Hocus pocus!" I roared at the black shadow slinking behind AnnaBell. The cat snarled once, then vanished, frustration clear in its amber eyes.

Like so many things in Ninespire, Hocus and Pocus had changed. They weren't the nice cats that AnnaBell remembered. They had been turned into hairball-spitting monsters with fangs and claws.

"Get up," I begged AnnaBell. "We have to hurry. Hocus is here somewhere."

I knew how the cats' magic worked now. When Pocus disappeared, Hocus appeared, and vice versa. One of the cats was always visible. The other was always invisible.

"I can't!" AnnaBell cried. "I'm stuck!"

As she said the words, she struggled wildly on the floor like someone pinned in a wrestling match. Her arms and legs thrashed furiously, but the rest of her was stuck in place.

"Go, Gidget!" she barked, giving up and going completely still. "Get out of here!" Struggling had gotten her nowhere. Pocus' hairball kept her glued to the floor.

Kauch-th-hu! Kauch-th-hu!

Now it was Hocus' turn, and the cat attacked faster than I could have imagined. Out the corner of my eye, I briefly spotted a blur of pouncing orange fur. Then a pair of slimy hairballs sloshed toward me, one right after the other.

"I'll be back!" I shouted, starting to run. I couldn't help AnnaBell then, and I had to save myself. Getting myself glued to the floor wouldn't do anyone any good.

I dodged right and then jumped left. Hairballs filled the air like gooey missiles from my slingshot. Some splattered wetly on the floor. Others splashed against furniture and kitchen tools.

Splab! Sklurk! Sploog!

"Hocus ... *p*-pocus," I panted, zigzagging across the kitchen floor. Sticky spray drenched my clothes and hair, but Hocus vanished with a snarl.

Gasping for breath, I rounded a corner and threw myself against a wooden crate. In my shrunken size, I thought it looked as big as a log cabin.

I bent over with my hands on my knees, gasping for breath. Hocus was gone, but Pocus was close. I had only seconds to rest before she found me.

"Wizard Ast, where are you?" I whispered hopelessly.

Simon and AnnaBell had been captured and I was on the run. I needed the wizard more than ever.

Thwoon-thwoon! Thwoon-thwoon!

Suddenly my heart started to pound again, like it had after the explosion outside. But it sounded as if it were beating inside of my skull instead of my chest.

"What's happening to me—?" I started to shriek. Then Pocus attacked.

Wheh-h-h-hhhhh!

The cat leaped from the top of the crate behind me, twisting in mid-air the way only cats can do. Her angry eyes bored into mine. Her hiss turned into a sharp gulp of air.

A hairball was coming, and Pocus had me right where she wanted me. I knew that sound.

Desperate, I sucked in a quick breath. It was a race, me against the cat. The first one to exhale would win.

"Hocus—" I started to scream.

Kauch ... Pocus readied her hairball.

"—po—" I went on, screeching now.

Th-hu!

Pocus spit before I could finish, heaving a hairball straight into my gut. The air exploded from my lungs and turned my screech into a groan.

I doubled over in pain, seeing stars. Even if I'd had the breath, I couldn't have screamed anymore. It took all of my willpower just to stay on my feet.

But I'm not sure why I bothered. I couldn't defend myself like that. I couldn't keep Pocus away.

Sure, I tried. I slapped my hand weakly at the cat's nose. I stumbled one way, then another, shuffling woodenly like a zombie.

Nothing I did made a difference. Pocus crouched, watched me patiently until the time was right, and then pounced.

Her big paw was the last thing I saw. It slapped against the side of my head, and the light in the kitchen dimmed. The world started to spin, and then darkness swallowed everything.

"Move!" she gasped. "I was wrong! The cats aren't nice anymore."

I knew immediately what had happened to Hocus and Pocus. Ninespire's madness had struck them, too.

Happy Baby or Not

18

Back and forth, back and forth. That was what woke me. I was swaying from side to side like laundry hung out to dry on a wiggly clothesline wiggling in the wind.

At first the sensation was soothing. I swayed gently, feeling lighter than air. My feet swished from left to right and back again. I was floating.

My eyes popped open at the thought. *Floating?* That didn't make sense.

"*W*-what?" I mumbled drowsily, trying to understand where I was and what was happening.

The unexpected sight of thick orange fur and a cat's collar explained everything. They were inches from my face and could mean only one thing.

Hocus was carrying me!

Rusty buckets! was my first thought. *I sure hope no one sees me like this* quickly followed. Hocus had a tight grip on my backpack, and I dangled from his mouth like a kitten clutched by the scruff of its neck.

Being captured by a giant monster-cat was one thing. Being toted around like a baby was something else. How embarrassing!

But right away I thought I had a solution. *Just say* hocus pocus. *The cat will disappear,* I reminded myself.

It was almost too easy, and I couldn't believe that I had worried. Neither of the cats could keep me prisoner for long. I knew their weakness.

"Hocus …" I started to whisper. Then an awful memory came to mind and I snapped my mouth shut.

I saw mouse-Simon struggling in Pocus' clutches. His tail was pinned beneath the cat's paw. His eyes were wide and full of tears.

Then he and Hocus had vanished. Why? Because Simon had said *hocus pocus.* And when the cat had reappeared, my friend hadn't. I could only imagine where he was.

So instead of shouting, I kicked my legs and flailed my arms. I even started to wail. I figured if someone were to see me being carried like a baby, I might as well act like one. At least I wouldn't look like a *happy* baby.

Nothing I did made a difference. Hocus didn't drop me or loosen his grip. My punches and kicks didn't land on anything but air.

Wherever the cat was taking me, I was going. Happy baby or not.

Finally, I gave up. At least I was alive, and I could hope the same for AnnaBell and Simon. Since Hocus hadn't gobbled me up, maybe my friends hadn't been eaten either.

At times Hocus carried me across plain floor stones. At other times, we passed over thick carpet or down twisting stairways. All I could do was wait and wonder when something would happen.

Castle Ninespire wasn't itself anymore. Weird and frightening magic roamed its halls. Something unusual was bound to come along soon, maybe a rain cloud pouring snapsoda fizz or a pair of goblins bowling with their heads.

Hocus miraculously avoided the dangers of Ninespire. I hoped that wasn't because he was dangerous enough himself.

By the time I was thinking about goblins bowling with *my* head, the cat dropped me. There was no warning or signal. Just—*spluck!*—onto the floor I went.

I bounced almost instantly to my feet, feeling furious. Hocus and Pocus should treat guests better than that, crazy castle or not. I wasn't a trespasser. I had been invited on official business.

I raised one finger for a scolding and rounded on what I thought was Hocus. But to my surprise, the orange cat was gone.

"Now you listen—!" I began.

Fliddle, flit-flit.

Instead of Hocus, something heavy and with dark wings

scudded over my head. I swallowed my words and threw myself onto my back to avoid being hit.

Hocus was gone, but a new monster had taken his place.

19

Leathery wings fluttered above my head, rustling like dry leaves swept over stone. They crowded the air like a flock of birds, and suddenly the creature I'd thought was alone had friends.

Fliddle, flit-flit. Fliddle-flit.

About ten of the creatures flapped awkwardly overhead. Their bindings creaked. Their yellowed pages—

My eyes did a double-take. *Bindings? Yellowed pages?* The creatures weren't creatures. They were books! They flew by flapping their covers like wings.

I jumped to my feet and crouched with my arms wide. The next book that came close was in for it. I'd tear it apart with my bare hands.

"Good boy," I purred as if coaxing a puppy in a game of fetch. Slowly a flying book fluttered nearer. "C'mere. Come to Gidget."

To myself, I added, *So I can pluck out your pages one by one!*

The book flew closer, its dry pages shuffling softly. I flexed my knees and cracked my knuckles, waiting.

"Gidget?"

An unexpected voice interrupted my concentration, and I rapidly spun around.

"Who is it?" I demanded. The voice wasn't familiar. It could be another Ninespire trick.

Unfortunately, my curiosity left me wide open to an attack.

Blump! A book smacked into the back of my head.

The surprise blow knocked me over and I went down like a circus clown tripping on her oversized shoes. I landed facedown on my nose. There was no chance to see who had spoken.

Rusty buckets! I complained, embarrassed. *Isn't acting like a fool AnnaBell's specialty?*

It wasn't nice to think about my friend like that, but things weren't exactly going my way. I was sure AnnaBell would forgive me.

"Gidget, you poor-unfortunate thing," the unfamiliar voice continued. "I've never seen you so tiny-small before."

Even with my nose mashed into the carpet, I blinked when I heard those words. They could belong to only one person. Only he would say something like "tiny-small" on

purpose.

"Wizard Ast!" I cheered, instantly forgetting the bad things that had happened recently. The wizard would make everything right. He would rescue my friends and turn Castle Ninespire back to normal.

"I'm so glad to see you," I blurted, leaping to my feet. "I've been looking all over … for …"

The words died on my lips. I took a step back. The person standing in front of me wasn't Wizard Ast. It was an imposter dressed in his clothes. It was a boy in a fake white beard!

Heart and Goal

20

"Where's Wizard Ast?" I demanded, pointing a finger at the imposter standing before me. "Who are you?"

Ninespire had gone mad, I reminded myself. Nothing in it could be trusted. Not pets, not golems, and certainly not a boy wearing a long white beard.

I mean, who ever heard of a six-year-old with a beard?

The imposter frowned and pushed up his sleeves. They were much too long for him, and extra material bunched at his elbows. He might as well have been wearing an adult's outfit.

"Look closer-deeper," he urged, still copying Wizard Ast's peculiar doublespeak. His piercing blue eyes narrowed seriously.

Something about that look made me pause. I changed my mind. That look was too familiar, and I was sure I'd seen those eyes many times before.

"Oh, Wizard Ast!" I nearly sobbed. "What's happened? Everything has gone crazy!"

Ninespire had struck again. Wizard Ast had been turned into a six-year-old boy. Not even he was safe from the castle's curse.

The boy-wizard smiled down at me, his face very face away. Seeing him look so tall reminded me that I was still only three inches high.

"Let's get you back to normal size-height," he said first, seeming to read my mind. Then he raised his arms, wiggled his fingers, and chanted a short rhyme.

From big-large to small
And back to size,
Grow quick-fast, be tall.
Stretch up and rise.

I started yawning and feeling sore as soon as he closed his mouth. First my legs ached as if they were in the middle of a growing spurt. Then my back and shoulders felt tight, so I raised my arms for a good long stretch.

Vrr-r-r-rooop!

As I stretched, I grew. It was that simple. When I lowered my arms, I was my normal-sized self again.

"That's an improvement-better," Wizard Ast declared. He now looked up at me instead of down. I was almost twice as tall as he was.

"*Th*-thank you," I said slowly, trying not to sound too

relieved. Sure, I was glad to be my regular size, but Wizard Ast was still six-years-old. Not everything was better yet.

"Now what about you?" I asked. "Can you … fix yourself?"

Wizard Ast cackled cheerfully. "*Fix* myself? Dear Gidget, I am not a broken-inoperative wagon wheel. I need-require magic, not repairs."

I squinted at him in confusion. He was a wizard, the best around. Who would know more about magic than he did?

"Don't you know the right spell?" I teased, wiggling my fingers in my most wizardly way.

"I wish it were that easy-simple," he replied somewhat sadly. "But I cannot undo-correct what has happened. Not until the experiment returns."

When he said the word "experiment," my heart started to pound again. Almost instantly, its unbearable noise caused my knees to buckle, and I slapped my palms over my ears.

Thwoon-thwoon! Thwoon-thwoon!

"Help me!" I gasped. "My heart is going to explode!"

That wasn't really how I felt, but the truth wasn't easy to explain. My heart *sounded* loud, but it didn't *feel* loud. In fact, I couldn't feel it at all. I doubt I would have noticed it if not for the noise.

Thwoon-thwoon!

"Please do something!"

Suddenly the wizard was there, pulling my hands from my ears. His eyes bored into mine. I'd never seen a more intense look.

"Do you hear it, too?" he demanded. Although he looked like a boy, he didn't sound like one. "Do you hear-perceive the experiment?"

I stared at him blankly, not understanding. *What experiment?* The pounding of my heart drowned out everything else. I couldn't hear any experiment.

Thwoon-THWOON! Thwoon-THWOON!

I wanted to scream and stuff cotton in my ears. Anything to stop the noise. It had been bothering me since the explosion. Since the fireball. Since—

The experiment.

Suddenly I understood. The noise I was hearing wasn't my heartbeat, and it wasn't coming from inside of me. It was coming from the fireball.

That was the experiment Wizard Ast was talking about. The fireball. I was hearing it pulse from miles away.

Thwoon-thwoon! Thoo—!

Now that I understood, I discovered that I could stop listening. The sound vanished when I wanted, and it re-turned when I tried to hear it again.

It's magic, I told myself. *There is something magical connecting us. Probably from when it passed through me.*

Finally I nodded to Wizard Ast. "Yes, I hear it," I whispered. "It's coming from that way." I raised my hand and pointed to the left. The fiery experiment was somewhere off in that direction.

"Wonderful-terrific!" the wizard beamed. "If you can follow it, you can catch-capture it and return!"

His words made sense to me immediately, and I couldn't keep from gulping. Wizard Ast wanted me to chase the missing experiment and catch it.

21

"Why me?" I groaned, feeling sorry for myself. Why did I have to chase a dangerous experiment? Gadgets were my specialty, not magic.

The wizard patted my shoulder. "I must stay-remain here," he explained. "My castle-home needs my attention."

I sighed dramatically. "Fine, I'll go. But there'd better be some kingbite cookies in it for me."

Actually I didn't mind helping. The idea sounded fun and adventurous. But I hadn't eaten dinner yet, and I wondered if a girl could be a hero on an empty stomach.

Apparently Wizard Ast didn't think so. He pushed up his sleeves again and cast another spell.

When the tummy-stomach rumbles,
Goblin-growls,
And loudly grumbles.

Spell some supper-dinner vittles.
Make a meal
To fill your middle.

He lowered his arms, and there came a startling noise behind me. It sounded like a herd of mooing cows tromping through a field.

Rusty buckets! I thought, fearing the worst from the castle. *I'm going to be trampled.* But when I spun around, I didn't see a single cow or sign of danger.

Instead I saw bread, butter, cheese, milk, and strawberry eatagones! Enough for a feast. They were spread out on Wizard Ast's desk as if it were a banquet table.

"I'm still working on the cookies," he admitted. His fingers twitched like a musician preparing to play.

I snorted happily. "Thank you, but this is plenty. I couldn't finish it all, not even with AnnaBell and Simon's—"

My head shot up in alarm. "AnnaBell and Simon! They're in trouble. Your cats have them!"

I couldn't believe that I'd forgotten my friends. What sort of fireball-chasing hero was I?

"Fear-worry not," Wizard Ast smiled. "Hocus and Pocus may seem unusual-odd, but they are loyal friends."

Right away, I wanted to disagree. The wizard obviously hadn't seen his cats recently. He didn't know that they were mean now.

"But …" I mumbled, spraying bits of cheese out of my mouth.

I blinked and quit trying to speak. My mouth was surprisingly stuffed with cheese, and my hands clutched fistfuls of slippery bread. Melting butter oozed through my fingers.

When did this happen? I wondered. I couldn't remember picking up any food. When had I crammed so much of it into my mouth?

"Yum-delicious!" Wizard Ast mumbled. His mouth sounded suspiciously full, but it was I who almost choked when I saw him.

He was hovering in the air over the desk like a hummingbird above a flower. His oversized robe dangled in the food. His hands greedily scooped up more than they could hold.

Blech!

Seeing Wizard Ast that way brought me to my senses. I spat the cheese out of my mouth and threw down the bread in my hands.

"No!" I wailed. "It's the castle. Ninespire is making … It's making …"

Suddenly I couldn't remember what I'd been saying. The food had my attention again. No matter how much of it we took or ate, there never seemed to be any less.

"The castle is making all of this yummy food!" I howled in delight. That wasn't what I'd intended to say, but I

96

started shoveling eatagones into my mouth anyway. I never wanted to stop!

Eating that way was wrong. All the burping, swallowing without chewing, taking more than I could finish. But even mighty Wizard Ast was gobbling like a goblin from a plate of stolen leftovers.

"So … *burp* … good," I belched, grinning gluttonously.

"I couldn't agree-concur more," Wizard Ast burped. "But don't consume-eat that. It's mine." With his chin, he indicated a buttery hunk of bread. It looked like the tastiest treat ever baked.

I didn't take my eyes from it. "I'll fight you for it," I said seriously. I meant it more than anything I'd said before.

Wizard Ast didn't hesitate. He balled a piece of cheese between his thumb and forefinger. Then he calmly took aim and flicked it at my nose.

Dirp!

I barely felt the attack, but it still meant war. Tinker versus wizard. It would be one for the history books.

I went for his beard first, yanking it. Then he snatched my goggles, pulled, and let go. *Splasp!* They slapped against my forehead, stinging and leaving a mark.

The fight got worse from there. Soon food started to fly, and insults, too. The whole thing was ridiculous.

"Milk mustache!" I yowled.

"Cheese bandit-thief!" countered the wizard.

"Butter beard!"

Of course I followed that by smearing butter into his beard. Sextuple yuck!

We might have gone on forever. The supply of food seemed endless. But the appearance of Hocus froze us in mid-insult.

The orange cat padded quietly into the room. From the cat's mouth dangled an unmoving tiny white shape.

"Simon!" I cried through a mouthful of food. "Simon, wake up!" When my friend didn't stir, I was sure he was dead.

Noble Reunion

22

"Hocus, drop him right now!" I ordered the cat. Now that I wasn't three inches tall, I wasn't so afraid of him.

But Wizard Ast was afraid. He saw something that I missed.

"Duck-get down!" he shouted. At the same time, he tugged on my belt and dragged me to the floor. For a six-year-old, he was strong!

Kauch-th-hu!

Hocus spat noisily, sending a gooey hairball hurtling through the air. It oozed over our heads and slapped wetly on Wizard Ast's desk.

Splerck!

Clumps of hair and moisture sprayed into the air. Then more hairballs started to fly. *Kauch-th-hu! Kauch-th-hu!* These, too, splattered onto the desk. *Splerck! Splerck-splerck!* What was the crazy cat trying to do?

"This is too weird!" I bellowed, struggling to untangle myself from Wizard Ast's oversized robe. "Let me get up!"

But the more I struggled, the tighter Wizard Ast held on.

"No, Gidget," he grunted between clenched teeth. "Let-allow Hocus to finish."

My muscles went slack when I heard that. The words stole the fight right out of me. Wizard Ast wanted Hocus to win. He was on the cat's side.

Ninespire has won, I thought, squeezing my eyes shut. I feared the worst. Hot tears trickled out and onto my cheeks. *Everything in it is against me.*

Even Wizard Ast.

With my eyes still closed, I heard him chanting softly. He was casting another spell, this one against me.

Sleep-rest,
Dream deep,
Start counting sheep.
Stir-wake
Next morn
When dawn is born.

His words whispered in my ears like the soothing sounds of a gentle rain. I tried to resist them, but their magic was too strong. In seconds, I was asleep.

I woke slowly sometime later. Sunlight streamed in from a window above me. Blankets were coiled around my legs the way Wizard Ast's robe—

I came fully awake, and everything else came back, too. Wizard Ast had used magic to put me to sleep. Why would he do that?

"Gidget, you're awake!" AnnaBell cried. She was sitting in a chair next to my bed.

"Gidgi, you 'wake!" Simon echoed, sitting in her lap. He wasn't a mouse anymore. He was back to being a three-year-old boy.

Seeing them, I lay back down, feeling overwhelmed. My friends were safe and Wizard Ast's spell hadn't done anything bad to me. In fact, I felt as rested as if I'd spent a peaceful night in my own bed at home.

"Are you all right?" AnnaBell asked, squinting at me. "Would a joke make you feel better?"

Thinking of her jokes, I shook my head. "No, no, I'm fine," I blurted quickly.

"It's no trouble," she smirked. "Anything to help a friend."

I groaned and pulled the blankets over my head. AnnaBell was acting exactly like her normal self. Lucky me.

"Where did the fortune teller learn to dance?" she quipped.

I whimpered beneath the blankets. There was no stopping her.

"At the crystal ball!" she hooted after a pause. "Bah-bah-boom! Good one, huh?"

"Sure," I said, lowering the blanket. "It was your best yet. Now can you tell me what's going on?"

My friend snorted. "Fine, be a grump. I won't tell you how Wizard Ast is going to get us out of here." She crossed her arms and turned her head.

"What?" I blinked, flailing my arms and sitting up again. "How?"

"Hmmph!" AnnaBell made a big show of ignoring me. She turned away so quickly that the bells on her cap jingled.

"Friends shouldn't argue-fight," Wizard Ast said, seeming to step out of thin air. *Hone Friendship until It Is Stronger Than Armor and Reaches Farther Than a Sword.*

Out of the corner of my eye, I saw AnnaBell wince. She recognized the words. They were from *The Noble Deeds and Duties*.

Both of us lowered our heads, ashamed. "Yes, Wizard Ast," we said at the same time.

"Good!" he beamed. "So, then, who wants to fly-ride out of here on a wizard's magic hat?"

When I heard that, I groaned again. Getting out of the castle was going to be as unpleasant as getting in.

23

"Jump-leap from this window," Wizard Ast advised.
"The angle-trajectory should see you safely to Tiller's
Field."

I sputtered when I heard that. *Should see us safely.* It
sounded too much like *maybe*, and I wondered what we
were getting ourselves into.

But the wizard continued as if jumping out of a window
was a perfectly ordinary thing to do. "Once you're in town,
find-locate the sheriff. He will gladly accompany-join you
on your quest."

Wizard Ast made everything sound easy, but I wasn't
convinced. He wanted AnnaBell and me to jump out of the
window while holding onto his hat. That was his plan.
Somehow the beat-up old hat was supposed to make us
float.

No wonder I liked gadgets. They made a lot more sense

than magic.

But before I knew it, AnnaBell and I were huddling outside on a window ledge on Ninespire's tallest tower. We clutched the brim of the wizard's hat in our sweaty hands. The ground was a long, long way down.

"Any *l*-last-minute advice?" I asked Wizard Ast nervously. He and Simon stood safely inside the tower.

The wizard shook his head. "Track the experiment and catch-nab it in my hat. I will meet-join you in Tiller's Field."

I listened doubtfully, thinking dark thoughts. *You forgot the part where we fall out of this window and get squished like grapes.*

Like I said, Wizard Ast made it sound too easy.

"Now say-recite the spell I taught you and go," he urged. "Simon and I will guard-protect the castle."

And that was that. AnnaBell and I had to find the experiment and catch it. Then Wizard Ast would use it to reverse the weird magic in the castle.

See how simple it was?

AnnaBell surprised me by starting the spell first.

Flutter by, butterfly,
Float right through the sky …

she chanted alone, and I had to think fast to catch up.

104

Flock of two cockatoos
Flap your wings on high.

We finished together and then held our breath, the hat stretched tight between us. Saying the spell had been easy. Now it was time for the hard part.

We had to jump.

I glanced down and my stomach rolled over. My scoot boots weren't going to save me from a fall this high.

I swallowed hard. "One," I whispered slowly.

"Three!" AnnaBell shouted mischievously. Then, with a giggle, she leaned sideways and dragged us off the ledge.

What happened to two*? I wanted to scream at her. *You were supposed to say* two*!*

But I couldn't speak. Air rushed into my lungs as if I were drowning in it. I could barely exhale.

"Goodbye, Simon! Goodbye, Wizard Ast!" AnnaBell cried fearlessly.

I just wanted to cry. *Goodbye, being alive!* We were falling. We were going to die. We were—

"Open your eyes," AnnaBell snickered. "You don't want to miss this."

"Miss what?" I barely managed to snarl. "Us being flattened like pancakes?"

In response, AnnaBell nudged my shin with her foot. "I'm not joking," she growled. "Look around!"

Still snarling, I reluctantly pried my eyes open. I couldn't let AnnaBell be brave alone. She was younger than I was.

To my astonishment, we weren't falling and it appeared we weren't going to die. We were floating like a fluffy dandelion seed caught in a gentle breeze.

Air filled Wizard Ast's hat, stretching it to giant size like a balloon. AnnaBell and I dangled from its floppy brim with our legs swaying slowly.

Color was everywhere. One shade of blue painted the sky. Another traced a path through the fields below. Greens and yellows identified growing things. Browns, greys, and reds showed where people had left their mark.

"It's ... breathtaking," I murmured, awestruck. The world was a rainbow that I wished everyone could see.

For several minutes, we enjoyed the scenery in silence. Castle Ninespire drifted away, and our home town, Tiller's Field, drew steadily nearer. Everything was peaceful until—

"Wheee-heh-heh-heee!"

Without warning, something small, fast, and loud zipped past us. It was a speeding blur of purple and brown.

"Now what?" AnnaBell groaned, and I shared her feelings exactly.

We'd had enough surprises already. Enough to last until we were old or adults, whichever came first.

"Get away from us!" I screamed. Any closer and the thing would have knocked us off the hat.

"Wheee-heh-heh-heee!"

The tiny flier ignored my warning and turned sharply in the distance to face us. There it hovered, seeming to take aim or size us up.

"Know any good jokes?" I asked AnnaBell hurriedly.

"*J*-jokes?" she stuttered. "You want to hear jokes *now*?"

I shrugged. "It might take our minds off falling."

Her eyes went wide with fear. "No, Gidget, don't. Don't even think about letting go."

Let go? I almost laughed. Not in a million years. Not even if I were being tickled. AnnaBell had made her best joke without even trying.

Ahead of us, the witch didn't laugh. Yes, the *witch*. That was what was flying around up here with us. I'd heard enough cackles on Cauldron Cooker's Night, a holiday for witches, to know what I was hearing.

"Wheee-heh-heh-heee!"

24

Cackling with glee, the witch sped toward us. She threw back her head and kicked her heels as if she were riding a horse.

"Wheee-heh-heh-heee!"

"What's *h*-happening?" AnnaBell asked, cringing on the other side of the hat. She was facing me and couldn't see the witch.

I sputtered, speechless. *What* is *happening?* I wondered. *What's wrong with that witch? She's not ... normal.*

No matter how much closer she came, the witch never seemed to get bigger. At least not as big as she should have gotten. She looked as small as—

A child.

My heart sank. The witch was a tiny person riding a tiny broom. She was a toddler, like Simon.

"Not again," I groaned. Ninespire's weirdness had

escaped the castle and was following us.

"What?" AnnaBell demanded. "'Not again' what?"

I smiled hugely, showing most of my teeth. I didn't feel like smiling, but what else could I do?

"We have to baby-sit again," I said, my voice syrupy sweet. Trying to be calm when you wanted to shriek wasn't easy.

"Babysit …?" AnnaBell repeated, slowly working out what I'd told her. Then her mouth made a surprised *O*-shape, and I knew she had it.

"Simon?" she asked.

Well, *almost* had it.

"Not him," I replied. "Someone else who knows magic." I paused to squint at the approaching witch. "Someone with blonde hair."

AnnaBell made a face at me. "How many wizard-type people do we have in town? It has to be Jozlyn."

I almost slapped myself. Jozlyn! I should have recognized her right away.

Jozlyn was an enchantress, which is a fancy name for female wizard. She was also one of the kid heroes of Tiller's Field. Almost every girl in town wanted to be just like her.

At least they did when she wasn't two- or three-years-old. Jozlyn was supposed to be a teenager.

"Wheee-heh-heh-heee!" she cackled at the top of her little lungs. She was almost on top of us.

"What happened to you?" I shouted at her. Of course I already knew. Ninespire had happened. I was just trying to get her to slow down.

Swackt!

Jozlyn didn't answer. She swatted my foot as she passed instead. Then, from over her shoulder, she dared us to follow.

"Tag! You it!" she hooted, sticking out her tongue.

"Rusty buckets!" I snarled. "Now what?" We couldn't leave a two-year-old alone outside. Especially one flying around on a miniature broom.

"Jump," AnnaBell said with no hint of a joke.

I looked at her and crossed my eyes. "Funny, funny. That's your best ever."

She ignored my comment. "Jump," she repeated more firmly, and the tone of her voice alarmed me. I'd never heard her sound more serious.

"Why, what's—?"

"Now!" she roared. Then to my surprise, she spread her fingers and let go. It wouldn't be the last time she surprised me by letting go.

"AnnaBell, no!" I shrieked. But she fell in an instant. Without her on the other side, the hat lost control.

First it started to spin. Then it rocked crazily like a capsizing canoe. Confusing sights and colors flashed past me—greens, blues, browns, and a dusty grey like dry stone.

All I could tell was that the hat and I were going down.

110

We were going down fast.

I wanted to scream out loud. It seemed like the thing to do. But my stomach was in my throat, and I was too afraid to open my mouth.

So I screamed silently and without hope. I screamed to the howling of wind in my ears.

Scoot boots, don't fail me now!

But it was green that saved me. Green leaves and brown bark. A sea of wooden arms seemed to magically reach out and break my fall.

Thuh-blamp! "Ungh!"

Thah-blump! "Ow!"

I didn't say it was easy. I said the trees broke my fall. They did it eleven times, sending me bouncing and banging down to the ground. I know because I counted every bump.

Thwunt!

"Oooooh ... "

Landing hurt the most, and I didn't want to move afterward. I wasn't even sure I could.

But I found out in a hurry.

Thwoon-thwoon! Thwoon-thwoon!

Because the experiment picked exactly that time to return.

Dead and Death

25

"Get up, Gidget, get up!" I hissed, praying to be quick. The experiment was close and louder than ever. My choices were move or be squished.

Thwoon-thwoon! Thwoon-thwoon!

The experiment's pounding made my insides rumble like the contents of a boiling cauldron. Trees quivered and the ground quaked. Damp things fell into my hair from the branches overhead.

Can my luck get any worse? I wondered bitterly. The experiment was almost on top of me, and I had crash-landed in Everleaf Woods. Falling out of Wizard Ast's tower would have been safer.

Everleaf Woods was the second most deep, dark place I knew of. Only Croneswart Swamp was worse. The woods always let visitors in, but it didn't always let them out.

Forget the experiment, I told myself, thinking fast. *Just get out of the woods. Find a way out.*

Right then, that was the most important thing. The experiment and I were still connected, so I could easily track it later. But I wouldn't always remember the way out of Everleaf. The trees would see to that.

I took a deep breath, slapped down my goggles, and pushed myself up. There was no clear break in the trees, but one had to be near. I couldn't be more than a few dozen feet inside the woods.

GRAUNCH!

Make that a few dozen feet too far.

Screeching, the woods ahead suddenly split apart. Hundred-year-old trees toppled over, snapping in half. Dirt-covered roots erupted from the ground like skeletons clawing out of shallow graves.

Something terrible was coming, something as strong as an earthquake and as loud as a tornado. My guess was the end of the world.

Grr-rauwgh!

A terrible beast as tall as the trees smashed a path into the woods. The sharp sound of splitting timber shrieked around it. Fallen trees were piled high in its wake.

The monster was the corpse of something from long ago. It was half-wolf, half-dinosaur, and stood on two legs. Worms and weedy plants clung to its grey bones. Spikes as long as a knight's lance sprouted from its back like the quills on a porcupine.

The creature was dead and death. Only one thing could make it more horrifying.

The experiment.

Beating like a fiery heart in the monster's chest was the Ninespire Experiment. It pulsed with terrifying power. It had done the impossible. It had brought the dead back to life.

Grr-rauwgh!

26

In that instant, I froze and forgot about finding a way out of the woods. I forgot about running. I just stood there listening to the enormous drumbeat pound in my head.

Thwoon-thwoon! Thwoon-thwoon!

The sound was the sound of my death. *Thwoon-thwoon!* It matched my heartbeat. *Thwoon-thwoon!* It caused the ground to shudder as if it had been struck by a comet. *Thwoo—!*

"Gidget, run!"

AnnaBell got me moving. Soaking wet, she seemed to step out of thin air. The bells on her cap dangled limply against her forehead. A brief smile crossed her face.

"We've got you covered," she said breathlessly. "Run!"

Confused, I shook my head. "*W*-we …?" I mumbled.

AnnaBell winked and pointed overhead. There I spotted toddler Jozlyn riding her miniature broom.

"Wheee-heh-heh-heee!" she cackled, waving.

Wonderful! I thought. *I'm being rescued by a girl in bells and another in diapers! Whatever happened to knights in shining armor?*

S-s-s-splurgtt!

They had been zapped by crazed experiments, that's what.

Ahead of us, the monster raised its arms as if flexing its muscles. The fireball darkened in its chest like rapidly cooling lava, and then a thick crimson beam sprang from its center.

S-s-s-splurgtt!

AnnaBell and I dove in opposite directions, barely evading the attack. The beam splattered against a nearby tree, and what happened next shouldn't have surprised us.

The tree grew younger, shrinking as if doused with acid. Its bark became light and smooth. Its leaves shriveled on the branch, turning into buds or completely disappearing.

In seconds the whole tree was unrecognizable. A slender sapling shivered where the mature tree had so recently towered.

"Incredible," I murmured. Until then, I had only known what the experiment could do. I hadn't actually seen it in action.

But now I understood. Now I was terrified. The experiment could blast me into babyhood with one shot.

Our mission was doomed! We couldn't catch the experiment in Wizard Ast's hat like a butterfly in a net. We needed gadgets and powerful magic, not headgear.

"Rusty buckets!" I muttered over and over. We were beaten before we'd really gotten going.

"Don't just lie there," AnnaBell hissed from somewhere close. "I've still got a few tricks up my sleeves."

Just like that, she said exactly the right thing. I couldn't see her, but somehow she could reach my mind. Good friends, I think, can do that when they pay attention.

"All right," I said. "I'll go left and you g—"

A rustle in the bushes interrupted me. AnnaBell sprang from hiding and started to sprint toward the monster. She waved her arms and shouted jokes at the top of her lungs. She wasn't listening to me.

"What's the difference between a smelly experiment and the inside of my shoe? How many skeletons does it take to count to two hundred and six?"

She didn't shout punch lines, but she didn't need to. They weren't important. She was just trying to get the monster's undivided attention.

So that I can run away, I realized. AnnaBell was protecting me by putting herself in danger.

Thwoon-thwoon! Thwoon-thwoon!

The monster spotted her immediately, and the experiment beat louder. Blue and orange flames flared in the creature's hollow eye sockets. Steam hissed from the holes in its skull.

"Look out!" I howled, knowing what was coming next. The experiment was darkening again, and AnnaBell was an easy target.

27

S-s-s-splurgtt!

The monster raised its arms, and the experiment erupted again. Liquid fire streaked toward AnnaBell, bubbling and hissing loudly in the dense woods.

"Jump!" I wailed, realizing immediately how pointless that was.

Of course AnnaBell would jump. She didn't want to get hit. Not again. Not after being in Castle Ninespire when the experiment had started. She'd already been hit along with everything else inside.

But looking at her now, I couldn't tell that she had. She looked completely normal and was her regular age. She hadn't been turned into a frog, a toddler, or become an ugsud.

Then what had happened? I asked myself. *What had the experiment done to her?*

The experiment had changed everyone else in Ninespire—Simon, Mephello, Wizard Ast. It had even changed the whole castle. Didn't that mean that AnnaBell should have changed, too?

S-s-s-splurgtt!

There wasn't more time to wonder. The monster started to furiously hurl blast after blast at AnnaBell. Columns of fire briefly illuminated the woods like flashes of lightning.

S-s-s-splurgtt! S-s-s-splurgtt!

AnnaBell rolled one way and then cartwheeled another, staying one step ahead of the monster. She leaped and sprang like a water bug skimming over a calm lagoon. Her feet barely touched the ground.

She couldn't keep it up forever. Eventually she would make a mistake. One slip, one flubbed move, and the monster would have her. Luck didn't last.

"Go, AnnaBell!" I shouted, almost a cheer.

I had never been so proud of my friend, and I'd never felt more helpless. There wasn't anything I could do for her, not without more time.

That was the trouble with gadgets. They weren't as fast as magic or as unpredictable as a jester's acrobatics. They took time to build and required careful planning.

Give me an hour and I could have that skeleton's bones stacked neatly like a pile of firewood. But in a race through the woods, I was just a kid running for my life. The monster could finish me with one shot.

Knowing that, I realized that I'd never been closer to dying and that I'd never wanted to live more. I guess it can take danger to make us appreciate safety and comfort. It's funny how that works, and kind of sad.

S-s-s-splurgtt! The monster kept firing. *S-s-s-splurgtt!* And AnnaBell kept dodging.

Had the monster been attacking most anyone else, the contest would have ended already. But AnnaBell could jump, spin, twist, and tumble as well as I could tinker. She was safe until she got tired.

Don't let that be soon, I wished. *Please don't get tired, AnnaBell.*

"Time for act two!" she suddenly exclaimed, vaulting feet-first onto a low tree branch.

There she crouched expectantly like a timid bird ready for flight. She panted heavily, catching her breath, but was an easy target for the monster.

That was when Jozlyn came to the rescue.

"Wheee-heh-heh-heee!"

From the shelter of the thick leaves overhead, Jozlyn swooped down at the monster. For a two-year-old, she sure could fly. What a brave little girl!

Zrrrooowww! First she shot past the monster's eyes. *Vwwweee!* Then she raced behind its back. *Frrrwhoo!* And finally she zipped around its legs in a daring figure-eight.

Watching her almost made me dizzy. I could barely

believe my eyes. I certainly couldn't believe my luck. My friends were the best and bravest in the world.

AnnaBell and Jozlyn had risked their lives to save mine. They had put themselves in danger and acted like heroes so that I could escape. How could I ever thank them enough?

By doing what they want, I decided. And that was run. My friends were giving me time to escape.

So I did what they wanted and ran like a coward. There was nothing wrong with that. Running from a giant skeleton was perfectly normal. Trust me.

Besides, cowards usually lived to fight another day.

Boots stomping, I charged wildly through the woods. I paid little attention to where I was going. I watched my feet instead.

Fallen logs and branches seemed to try to trip me as I passed. Briars, thorns, and twisted roots caught my clothes like the bony fingers of the undead.

I had heard dark rumors about Everleaf Woods. Rumors that said its trees were unfriendly. But I'd never been deep enough inside to find out if they were true. I'd never really believed them until today.

And now I didn't want to believe or know the truth. Now I just wanted out.

Not much farther, I promised myself. *The edge of the woods is close. You're almost—*

Wampfh!

I crashed into something large and very solid. It felt like

a tree, or maybe a misplaced boulder. Either way, the blow sent me reeling onto my backside.

I landed hard and glanced at what I'd struck. When I saw it, I shrieked. My visit to Everleaf Woods had just gotten even more dangerous.

The object wasn't a tree or a boulder. It was another monster.

"Hallo, leedle peeples," it said, drooling heavily.

Big vs. Smart

28

The monster could talk! That scared me more than anything else about it.

Yes, the monster was almost as tall as two adults. Yes, it had tusks as long as my arms. And yes, it was clutching an uprooted bush the size of toddler Simon. It was even chomping on it as if it were a serving of cotton candy.

Those things were bad. But the monster's ability to speak was more terrifying. It meant that the creature wasn't just a brainless brute with oversized muscles. The monster was smart, too.

It was easy to be confused by big. But I knew that smart was always more dangerous than size. By itself, big couldn't tie its shoes. There was no reason to fear that.

So when the monster spoke, I panicked. Big and smart were a dangerous combination.

"Stay away *f*-from me," I blurted. "I have powerful

friends. Wizards and witches. They'll turn you into a toad."

I meant Wizard Ast and Jozlyn. Even though they wouldn't hurt anyone, the monster didn't know that. I was hoping the toad part would scare it away.

It didn't.

The monster blinked and cocked its head like a dog listening to a far-off sound. Its chewing slowed, and I imagined gears clunking in its thick skull.

"Yous is friends with Zeila Witch?" it said wetly, still drooling.

Now it was my turn to blink. The monster knew Zeila? She was a dangerous witch who lived in Croneswart Swamp. Her home was a hut built on eight spidery stilts.

Moving slowly, I pushed myself to my feet. I had a new plan now, one involving the witch. My eyes never left the monster's, and I tried to look threatening.

"Yes, I know her," I lied. "And she'll do whatever I ask, so you'd better let me go."

Actually, I had never seen or spoken to the witch, and we certainly weren't friends. But, again, the monster didn't know that. I was gambling.

The creature scrunched its bushy eyebrows together. "Mougi no likes Zeila Witch," it slobbered. "You leave—"

Whatever it had been about to say was lost in a sudden squeal. Jozlyn shot from the cover of the trees like a startled bird, squawking one word again and again.

"Moo-ee! Moo-ee! Moo-ee!"

I guess she was excited.

To be honest, I was excited, too. I'd heard of Mougi. He was a friendly ogre and had helped Jozlyn before. He was also a vegetarian and very polite in an ogrish sort of way.

"Jozlyn!" he blubbered, reminding me of a homesick puppy.

Right then, I realized that Castle Ninespire had changed me, too. I thought differently now and couldn't always tell a friend from a foe. What an awful thing.

AnnaBell stumbled from the trees next, her face red and sweating. Her jester's costume was wrinkled and stained with sap.

"Gidget?" she panted, spotting me first. Then, "Jozlyn?" And finally, *"Mougi?"* Her jaw dropped at least as far as mine had.

That did it. I tossed my arms up over my head. "Wait a minute! Does everyone here know everyone else except me?"

The three of them stopped what they were doing and stared at me. "Yes," they said at exactly the same time.

It sounded as if they'd practiced together, and I couldn't hold back a laugh. AnnaBell was always working on perfecting timing. It was the combination of how and when to tell a joke. Who knew she'd find it with an ogre and a baby enchantress?

Everyone laughed, and then Jozlyn introduced Mougi to

me. Before I could say, "Nice to meet you," he grabbed me in a crushing bear hug.

"Yous will protect Mougi?" he asked seriously. "The walking bones made Mougi small."

I balked at that. *Walking bones.* Did he mean the monster with the experiment stuck in its chest?

Jozlyn nodded excitedly. "Spine-soar Wreck," she agreed.

AnnaBell squinted at her. "Do you mean Spinasaurus Rex? Is that its name?"

Now Jozlyn made a face. "I said that already!"

I took that little outburst as a *yes*.

The monster was a Spinasaurus Rex. At least that had been its name when it was alive. Now that it was dead, we had to find a way to stop it.

29

"Mougi, you're hurting her!" AnnaBell said sharply. "Put her down!"

I nodded urgently, realizing that the ogre still had me in a bear hug. My world was quickly turning black, and I feared that the last thing I would ever see would be Mougi's drooling mouth.

The ogre sighed and let go, dropping me. He hung his blockish head.

"Leedle Mougi is sorry," he sniffed, reaching out to pat me with a meaty paw. "Even his brain is small."

Had I not been gasping for breath, I would have laughed. Little Mougi? Ogres weren't the smartest people, but nothing about Mougi was small.

"The Rex made you young," I said, figuring out what had happened. "The walking bones, I mean."

That was it. Mougi wasn't little. He was young. The

experiment had turned him into a child. For an ogre, he probably felt like a tiny baby.

The ogre nodded sadly. "Now Mougi can't snap every tree or smoosh every rock. Mougi is too little."

I tried to hide a look of relief. Snapping trees and smooshing rocks sounded dangerous. I wasn't sorry that he couldn't do those things at the moment. He had nearly smooshed me. What if he had been full-size?

"We'll fix you, Mougi," AnnaBell interjected. "Gidget and I are on a mission to stop the walking bones. Want to come with us?"

Hearing her question, I rolled my eyes. *Why not?* I thought sarcastically. We'd already spent time with two toddlers and a kid wizard. Having an ogre along couldn't be any worse.

"Sounds great," I fibbed, secretly crossing my fingers. I had a suspicion that it would be worse, and soon.

"But what about Sheriff Logan," I asked. "Wizard Ast told us to find him." The sheriff, I hoped, would keep Mougi from causing too much mischief. I liked the idea of teaming up with the sheriff instead of the ogre very much.

Jozlyn floated in close and shook her head. "Nuh-uh," was all she said.

"What do you mean?" I asked. "Did something happen to him, too?"

This time Jozlyn nodded. She spun her broom around, kicked her heels, and started scooting back into the trees.

Then she peered back at me from over her shoulder, and I got the idea that I was supposed to follow.

I waved for AnnaBell and Mougi to join me, then started after Jozlyn. The trees around us thickened immediately, so keeping up wasn't easy. Everleaf Woods was at it again.

"Slow down, please," I called. "Your broom is too fast."

Almost before the words left my mouth, Jozlyn wheeled around and zipped back to face me. She jerked to a stop inches from my nose.

"Peggy-sis," she said, sounding irritated.

"Huh?" I gasped. Had she meant *pegasus*? What did a magical horse have to do with anything?

"Not broom," Jozlyn continued gravely. "Peggy-sis."

Before I could argue, AnnaBell nudged my ribs. "Jozlyn won't ride a broom," she whispered. "She's not a warty old witch, remember?"

My eyes widened in understanding. It all made perfect sense. Jozlyn was *pretending* that her broom was a pegasus. Two-year-olds could get away with that sort of thing.

As a teenager, Jozlyn would never ride a broom. It just wasn't her style. Witches rode brooms, knights rode horses, and heroic kids rode wild creatures like pegasi, dragons, and griffins.

To be honest, I couldn't blame her. I'd rather not ride something my grandma used to sweep the floor. A fire-breathing dragon was more my speed.

"And what's your pegasus' name?" I asked her, playing along.

"Peggy," Jozlyn replied without batting an eye. I really should have seen it coming.

"Lead on," I told her, holding back a chuckle. Peggy the pegasus. AnnaBell had better remember that one for a future punch line.

Jozlyn guided us through a tangled stretch of trees, and then we suddenly stepped out of the woods. Traveling through Everleaf was like jumping into a deep pool. You were either safe or in over your head.

We exited near Gurgleburp Creek. That was a small, steady stream that separated the woods from Tiller's Field. My house was downstream, but I couldn't see it from here.

What I could see was a nightmare, and I fell to my knees at the sight. My hometown was in ruins and its buildings were burning.

30

Smoke filled the sky, and soot blackened the streets. Flames flickered in open windows and doorways.

Everywhere I looked, I saw destruction. The Tiller's Field I knew was gone, and my home would never be the same.

"*H*-how did this happen?" I gasped, sobbing. But I already knew. There was only one answer. Only one thing could have caused so much damage.

The experiment.

Now that it was out of Castle Ninespire, the experiment had changed. It wasn't just pulling annoying pranks and turning people into children anymore. It was destructive, even deadly.

AnnaBell placed a hand on my shoulder. "Let's get that thing," she growled.

Her thoughts echoed mine exactly. We could try to save

our town in one of two ways. We could help it now and let the experiment escape. Or we could capture the experiment first and fix everything later.

Even though I wanted to help now, that feel-good choice wasn't the right one. Many times it wasn't. Helping our town first wouldn't stop the experiment. That would allow it to get farther away, and mean more damage would be done.

So I took a deep breath, made my tough choice, and faced Everleaf Woods. My friends crowded around me, but I hardly noticed. I was concentrating on something else.

Thwoon-thwoon.

The experiment's heartbeat came to me softly as if echoing from very far away. But it came quickly and without delay. The two of us were still connected.

Thwoon-thwoon. Thwoon-thwoon!

Its beating gained strength, pounding ever louder. Soon it was all I could hear, and it felt close enough to touch.

"That way," I said firmly, pointing into the trees. I knew exactly where the Rex and its experiment-heart had gone. I could follow them anywhere.

"Jozlyn, what are you and Peggy going to do?" AnnaBell asked, grinning only a little.

Jozlyn smiled but shrugged. "Haffa protec' Joss," she explained.

After listening to Simon, translating Jozlyn's toddler-talk came easily. She had to stay behind to protect her brother

Josh. Normally he was a couple of years younger than she, but who knew now?

We said goodbye. Jozlyn scooted off across Gurgleburp Creek toward Tiller's Field. The water explained AnnaBell's wet clothing. She had fallen into the creek after letting go of Wizard Ast's hat.

Speaking of the hat, I tucked it into my toolbelt and started toward the woods. AnnaBell and Mougi followed close behind.

"Don' leeb Mougi," he pleaded. Some big tough ogre he was.

We walked through the woods for hours, tripping and stubbing our toes often. Only Mougi never tripped, plodding along as if walking down a clear street. A few roots and rocks couldn't hurt his frying pan-sized feet.

Strange noises echoed here and there like half-heard whispers. Some sounded utterly inhuman. There were growls, hisses, and the cracks of breaking things, too. Once we thought we heard the shuffling of clumsy feet behind us.

To make matters worse, night came early in Everleaf. The trees didn't allow much light through at midday. In the evening, the woods became as dark as a tomb.

Finally, I gave up. Branches I couldn't see swatted me left and right. All ten of my toes were throbbing from being stubbed. It was time to rest for the night.

"We'll camp here," I announced, stopping.

Mougi bumped into my back. AnnaBell bumped into his.

It was really getting dark!

"Camp?" AnnaBell exclaimed. "Here?"

By her tone, I could tell that she thought I was crazy. We were in the middle of Everleaf Woods. No one camped here.

But we couldn't keep walking in the dark. Sooner or later one of us would break an ankle. The smart thing to do was to wait for morning.

I found a clear, flat spot on the ground, and set my pop tent down in the middle of it. Most people have heard of a *pup* tent, but a *pop* tent is different. A pop tent starts out looking like an ordinary brick.

"Stand back, please," I told my friends. I set the brick down. Then I pressed the button on top of the tent and quickly backed away.

"One … two … three!" I counted.

Splorng! The pop tent did the rest.

The brick popped open, and the springs and gears inside it worked like a jack-in-the-box. But instead of a springy clown, a four-person tent burst out, ready for use.

Or in this case, a two-girl-and-one-ogre tent.

"Not bad, huh?" I boasted, smiling at the tent. It was another one of my inventions, and I never went far without it.

AnnaBell and Mougi scampered inside. "Hurry," AnnaBell called. "You're letting mosquitoes in."

I rolled my eyes. That was some thanks.

"How about some light?" she suggested after I was inside. Then she pulled three juggling balls from a pocket in her costume. "Simon taught this to me."

She cupped the balls in her hands and held them close to her lips. Then she whispered a curious rhyme.

Sunshine, lightning, firefly.
Daytime, stormy, nighttime sky.
Darkness vanish, fading—bye!
Rising, waking, morning's nigh.

When she said the word *nigh*, the balls in her hands started to glow—one red, one blue, and one purple. Their light wasn't strong, but it brightened the tent.

"Nice trick," I congratulated her.

"Mougi not so scared now," the ogre added. Still, the big lunk scooted closer to me.

AnnaBell smiled and bowed her head. "Now I'll *really* show you something."

With that, she started to juggle. The balls flashed in the air like playful fireflies. Their colors sparkled and danced. It was one of the prettiest displays I'd ever seen.

And one of the most terrifying.

A strange feeling came over me as I watched. Or maybe it was an *un*feeling. That's because I felt nothing—not hungry, not sleepy, not warm or cold. I felt … dead.

I knew I wasn't breathing either, but I couldn't open my mouth. My lungs wouldn't work, and not a single muscle in my body would budge.

AnnaBell, stop! I wished I could shriek. But it was useless.

Watching AnnaBell's juggling balls had paralyzed me. I was frozen!

A Glitch in Time

31

No more! I wailed silently. *Stop!*

AnnaBell's juggling had trapped me in a lonely place. I couldn't move, breathe, or speak. I watched the world as if I were a face in a portrait.

"Aren't you going to applaud?"

The words came out of nowhere like an unexpected whisper. They belonged to AnnaBell, but it took a moment for me to realize that.

"Huh?" I gasped, rubbing sandy eyes. I felt as if I were waking from a heavy afternoon nap. My head felt fuzzy and plugged.

"You know, clap for my juggling," AnnaBell grumped, sounding put out.

She was standing in front of Mougi and me. In her hands she clutched seven glowing balls. *Seven*, not the three I remembered.

That confused me. Where had the three extra balls come from? And when had AnnaBell stood up?

"I don't ... what ...?" I couldn't form my thoughts into words. They were too jumbled and my lips were too clumsy.

"Mougi slept with open eyes," the ogre stated. He said it casually, as if sleeping that way were normal.

AnnaBell frowned. "You mean I bored you?" she asked somewhat defiantly.

"Uh ..." Mougi didn't have a reply, and he desperately looked to me for help.

Luckily I understood what he'd said. *Slept with open eyes.* That was exactly how I'd felt while AnnaBell had been juggling.

"He's right," I agreed, nodding at Mougi. Then I looked at AnnaBell. "That's how I felt, too. Asleep with my eyes open."

This time AnnaBell shrugged with a snort. "Fine, fine. You don't like my juggling, tell me. I won't—"

"No." I cut her short. "You were good. Maybe so good that something else happened."

The words changed her attitude. "What do you mean?" she asked.

"Those balls might be magic," I said, thinking out loud. "Maybe the spell Simon taught you does more than make things glow."

"Well, that's easy to find out," AnnaBell replied. "I'll

141

juggle something else."

With a rustle of fabric, the balls disappeared into her pockets. She replaced them with three ordinary apples.

"All right," she said. "Watch closely and tell me if you see anything weird. Here goes."

She flicked her right arm and tossed an apple into the air. It arced near her forehead and then …

"Gidget!"

I blinked, feeling disoriented. "*W*-what? Why are you yelling?"

AnnaBell knelt in front of me. Her apples lay scattered on the tent's floor. Her wide eyes were wild.

Funny, I thought dreamily, *I don't remember her kneeling.*

"You stopped breathing!" she exclaimed. "You both did. For at least five minutes!"

I shook my head, trying to clear it. "Five minutes? What are you talking about? You were going to juggle the apples."

She jumped up, flailing her arms. "I did! That's what I'm saying. And you didn't blink the whole time. Mougi didn't even drool."

I caught my breath in surprise and fear. I'd been right. AnnaBell's juggling *had* frozen us. And I'd been right to wonder about what the experiment had done to her.

Because it had changed her. Something had changed inside her. Instead of making her young or turning her into something weird, the experiment had given her a new power.

When she juggled, she cast a powerful spell. A time-stopping spell. It froze anyone who watched her.

"Keep your hands at your sides," I told her. "I think I know what's going on."

She ignored me and bent to scoop up her fallen apples. "Just let me pick—"

"Stop!" I shouted, kicking an apple out of reach. "Don't move."

I glanced seriously at Mougi. "Hold her arms if you have to," I ordered.

The ogre frowned, and I couldn't blame him. He didn't want to treat AnnaBell like a criminal.

But we didn't have a choice. She was dangerous now. The experiment had given her a power that could stop an ogre in his tracks. We had to stop her before she used it again.

32

"What's the big idea?" AnnaBell exclaimed.

"Mougi is sorry!" the ogre apologized. "Mougi is very sorry."

His powerful hands clutched her upper arms and held her in the air. She kicked and complained loudly in his grasp.

"Put me down!"

Feeling guilty, I quickly snatched the apples up from the floor. It wasn't AnnaBell's fault that the experiment had made her dangerous, but we couldn't be too careful.

"All right, set her down," I finally said. "She can't juggle without apples."

Mougi did as I asked, and AnnaBell went rapidly to work. She started pulling ball after ball from her pockets.

Rusty buckets! I snarled inwardly. *You forgot about those.*

"Grab her again, Mougi!"

AnnaBell turned as Mougi jumped. Her hands rose, preparing to juggle. His fingers stiffened, reaching for her as he hurtled through the air.

Uh-oh! I thought, slapping my goggles down and looking away. Twice was enough. I couldn't allow myself to be caught a third time by AnnaBell's new power.

"Don't you see what you're doing?" I pleaded with her. "You're freezing us. You're turning us into statues."

That was it, AnnaBell's power. She could stop time nearby. Those who watched her juggle were frozen. They became stuck in time.

"*Y*-you're right, Gidget," she stammered, disbelief in her voice. "Look at Mougi."

I turned without thinking and terror struck. AnnaBell was still juggling, and I was staring right at her!

"What are you doing?" I shrieked, covering my eyes. In the process, I almost knocked off my goggles.

"Nothing," AnnaBell shot back defensively. "I said look at Mougi, not at me."

But I hadn't looked at Mougi. I had looked at her. I'd seen her arms whirling and balls flashing above her head. I'd seen her juggling.

Why, then, hadn't I been frozen?

I sneaked a look between my fingers like an impatient child playing peek-a-boo. AnnaBell was still juggling. Her small face was set in concentration.

Amazingly, I could blink and breathe and move. The

juggling wasn't affecting me.

"Must be your goggles," AnnaBell surmised. "I bet they protect your eyes."

Hearing her, I bit my lip. I was supposed to be the thinker. She was the jester. I should have realized that my goggles were protecting me.

Still, what a remarkable discovery! I was immune to AnnaBell's juggling. All I had to do was wear my goggles. That could definitely come in handy.

"Can I stop now?" AnnaBell asked. "Mougi is going to be sore."

Poor Mougi! He was still frozen. His arms were rigid and thrust out in front of his chest. He was balanced on one foot like a ballerina. His tongue stuck out between his tusks.

"Please!" I yelped, seeing him.

Flaump!

The ogre flopped stomach-first onto the floor as soon as AnnaBell quit juggling. He didn't bother to get up.

"Mougi felled down," he stated unnecessarily. "Must be time for sleepin'. Goodnight, leedle peeples."

In seconds, he was snoring.

AnnaBell and I just shrugged at each other. Mougi had the right idea. It was late and we'd done all that we could that day. We might as well sleep.

In the morning, Mougi rose first. "Who's hungry?" he bellowed, waking us.

146

"Me … maybe," I muttered. I wasn't really, not yet. But I thought it wise to agree with a bellowing ogre.

We packed my pop tent and then ate as we walked deeper into Everleaf Woods. Mougi provided us with a seemingly endless supply of mushrooms, and not one made me gag.

Mougi's mushrooms were different than most. They tasted like everything *except* mushrooms. White-speckled green ones tasted like gumdrops. Pink and white ones tasted like strawberry eatagones.

After eating one of Mougi's mushrooms, I couldn't get enough. Neither could AnnaBell and Mougi. Our hands dipped into Mougi's bag again and again, eager to sample new tastes.

"Blueberry-toogood," I said, chomping a flaky dark blue mushroom.

"Peppermint," AnnaBell hiccupped.

"Yummy pinecone," Mougi said with a loud crunch.

I glanced at him. "That *is* a pinecone," I said, trying to keep a straight face. Mougi had popped a real pinecone into his mouth!

"Yup," grinned the ogre. "Mougi knows. There's lots to share."

AnnaBell and I made faces at the suggestion. "No thank you!" we chimed politely.

Eating the mushrooms was fun, exciting, and full of surprises. We never knew exactly what flavor we'd get until we took a bite. And we were never disappointed.

At least we weren't until the bog hogs attacked. That was one surprise we could have done without.

GROFNK!

33

Soon the ground became damp and squishy. Frothy pools of dirty water appeared, and muck caked our shoes. A moist stench of rotting things gurgled up from beneath our feet.

"The swamp must be close," AnnaBell panted. Her dainty slippers *sclooped* and *glurped* in the sticky mud.

Mougi took a mighty sniff of the foul air. "Not far," he agreed. "I smell jellybelch."

Disgusted, I shuddered at the thought.

There were grisly creatures in Croneswart Swamp. Creatures with suckers and blind bulging eyes. Some of them slithered. Some of them limped on stunted limbs. All of them were hungry.

"There!" AnnaBell suggested, pointing at a cluster of mud-packed mounds. "Let's try those."

I liked the idea instantly. The mounds looked drier than

the ground and would give us a better view of what was ahead.

"Let's go!" I exclaimed, slogging forward.

AnnaBell beat me to the first mound and scampered up. I followed her closely, and Mougi rumbled up behind.

The mound was oblong and about the size of an ox used to plow fields. Dozens of similar mounds crowded the banks of Croneswart Swamp. Dark, thick water undulated as far as the eye could see.

"Time to doggy paddle," AnnaBell joked half-heartedly.

"Let's take a closer look," I said, shaking my head. I couldn't believe the experiment had gone into the water. "Maybe we won't have to—"

GROINK!

An ear-splitting sound that was half-squeal and half-roar cut me off. Sudden movement surged in the swamp, and the mound beneath us trembled violently.

GROINK! GRR-OINK!

The mounds were alive!

Squealing, they pushed themselves up from the muck on squat powerful legs. They shook like wet dogs, spraying mud. Their beady brown eyes burned with anger.

"Bog hogs!" Mougi roared, losing his balance and falling.

The creatures resembled giant wild boars but were made of mud and wet clay. Thorny plants sprouted from their backs like tentacles and coarse hair.

"They're disguised!" I cried, dismayed.

When hunkered down in the mud, they looked like ordinary mounds. The plants helped to make the disguise believable.

"This way!" AnnaBell shouted, clasping my arm.

With a yank, she dragged me from the back of the hog. We splashed into a churning pool and rolled rapidly to avoid being squished.

GRR-OINK! GROINK!

"We're … *g*-going to be … crushed!" I gasped between mouthfuls of swampy water. Either that or we'd drown in the pool.

But AnnaBell wasn't finished being a hero. She grabbed my backpack and hauled me onto dry land. I swear she was as nimble as a cat and had more lives!

From there, we darted right, then left, then back again. Sometimes we ran, sometimes we crawled. Everywhere we went was muddy and wet.

Enraged bog hogs swarmed us like a panicked crowd trying to escape a fire. Hooves churned. Squeals pierced our ears. Bulky bodies crashed and thrashed and threatened to mash us into pulp.

I felt as if we'd been plunked down in the middle of a cattle drive. *GROINK! GRR-OINK!*

Exactly how we escaped the herd, I can't remember. We broke free like fortunate swimmers clawing up from dark depths. Our lungs heaved, desperate for air.

Still in the middle of the herd, Mougi flailed his arms and

kicked his hairy feet. He was a tornado of muscle and speed. Every one of his blows splattered a muddy hog into a messy pile of muck.

"Run, leedle peeples!" he shouted at us. "Scurry on your teeny feets!"

AnnaBell and I glanced at each other, thinking the same thing. "No!" we shouted together. We refused to leave Mougi in danger.

"Loyalty Cannot Be Proven Too Often," AnnaBell added.

Her words were from *The Noble Deeds and Duties*, and they reminded us of how friends should behave. No matter how frightening the bog hogs were, Mougi deserved our help. He was our friend.

So we pushed up our sleeves and got ready to fight. We had bog hogs to squish and an ogre to rescue.

Slurp'n'Burp

34

"What's our plan?"

I asked the question quickly, but AnnaBell was already moving. Just as she had done in the laboratory filled with ugsuds, she sprinted into battle without fear.

And without me!

"No you don't!" I shouted after her, digging in the pockets of my tool belt. I knew just the gadget to take care of bog hogs. AnnaBell wouldn't be the only hero.

"Aha!" I cheered, finding my secret weapon. It was a long rubbery hose with a hand crank on one end.

I called the gadget a slurp'n'burp, and I usually used it for clean-up. Aim the nozzle, turn the crank, and the hose would slurp up almost any mess. Today I would use it to *make* a mess instead.

I sprinted for the swamp and let the hose unwind. When I reached the shoreline, I heaved one end of the slurp'n'burp into the water. While it sank, I charged back toward the bog hogs.

Mougi still thrashed among them. He was covered in slimy muck from head to toe. Had he not been so tall, I wouldn't have recognized him.

Splarp! His ham-sized fist slammed a hog. *Splurp!* His muddy foot connected with a second.

AnnaBell fought beside him. She gripped Wizard Ast's hat in one hand. Her other dipped into the hat again and again, pulling out the craziest things.

My eyes did a double-take. Wizard Ast's hat? I hadn't noticed her take it. She was even faster—and *trickier*—than I'd thought.

Out came her hand clutching a rubber chicken. "Don't get your feathers in a bunch!" she shouted, tossing the chicken at the nearest bog hog.

The swine barely slowed. It lowered its head and greedily gobbled the toy chicken in one gulp. The brief pause gave Mougi the time he needed.

Blomp! He smashed the hog with a mighty blow, splattering it like a warm meringue pie.

"That hog eats like a real pig!" AnnaBell exclaimed. She laughed as she stuck her hand back into the hat. What would she pull out next?

Still, my friends needed more firepower. Rubber chickens and a kid ogre wouldn't win the battle. The hat would eventually run out of surprises, and Mougi would eventually get tired.

Ten feet from the herd of hogs, I stopped running. I planted my feet, slapped down my goggles, and took aim. Then I started turning the slurp'n'burp's crank backward as fast as I could.

B-b-blurk! Swamp water erupted from its nozzle with a noisy belch.

"It's working!" I cried delightedly. I hadn't been too sure. Turning the crank backward was making the gadget work in reverse. Instead of slurping, it was burping!

Blur-r-rk!

A steady stream of bog water drenched the hogs. They squealed louder, crashing into trees, the swamp, and each other. All the while, they collapsed like melting snowmen.

"Who wants mud piggy pie?" I hooted, feeling pretty proud of myself. I was almost single-handedly stopping the herd.

But instead of cheering, Mougi waved his arms and pointed frantically behind me. "Run! Mougi told yous to run!"

Next to him, AnnaBell began to gesture just as urgently. Her eyes widened in terror.

"Gidget, behind you—look!" she wailed.

I spun around, and the slurp'n'burp slipped from my fingers. I wouldn't be needing it anymore, not against the creatures that were clawing up from the muck.

G-R-O-I-N-K!

An army of bog hogs rose from the mud. Together they bellowed like a dragon, blasting us with muddy spittle and breath that reeked of rotten cabbage. Septuple yuck!

"Run, leedle peeples!" Mougi pleaded again.

This time AnnaBell and I didn't have to be told. We were sprinting before the words left Mougi's mouth.

We knew when we were beaten. Gadgets and a wizard's hat wouldn't save us. The new herd was too big. All we could do was run for our lives.

G-R-O-I-N-K!

Arachno-Hut

35

"Over there!" I cried, stabbing a finger to our left.

A small wooden hut shaped like a tool shed peeked out from the trees ahead. It leaned slightly to one side on eight crooked stilts.

"It's got a door!" I added, meaning we could lock it behind us.

"Just go!" AnnaBell panted, meaning less talk and more running.

G-R-O-I-N-K! The bog hogs bellowed, meaning, *We're hungry and you're on the menu.*

We charged up to the hut and slid to a stop. A rickety ladder led straight to its door, but an odd orange and blue spider blocked our way. It hunched on the ladder's sixth rung.

"Be my guest," AnnaBell urged, indicating the ladder with a sweep of her arm.

"No, no," I said sweetly. "You first."

Neither of us wanted to face the spider. It was almost as big as an apple and had a strange triangular body, sort of like a witch's pointy hat. Octuple yuck!

"I'm not touching it," AnnaBell said finally, eyes on the spider. "I don't even like that thing you ride."

She meant my arachnoped riding machine. It had resembled a spider before being destroyed by the Ninespire Experiment. Now it was a worthless lump of scrap metal, far away.

G-R-O-I-N-K!

Another roar from the hogs decided it for me. I could either face the spider or wait for the herd of bog hogs. There really wasn't much of a choice.

I snatched my slingshot and scooped up a stone from the mud. But when I drew back and took aim, the spider was gone.

I paused, shrugging, then scrambled up the ladder.

"C'mon, chicken," I teased AnnaBell. Surprisingly she followed without making a joke.

The door to the hut creaked inward as if it hadn't been opened in years. Rust flaked from its hinges. Dust swirled in its opening.

"What is this place?" AnnaBell whispered, peering inside from over my shoulder.

I tried to answer her. I knew where we were. But something kept me from talking about it. My mouth wouldn't make a sound.

So I stepped inside with AnnaBell close behind. Our feet kicked up more dust, and the floorboards groaned beneath us.

"Maybe we were safer outside," I reconsidered. "Let's go back—"

Fwhemp!

Before I could finish, the door slammed shut behind us. This time it cackled like a witch instead of creaking.

Eh-heh-heh-heh-heh!

AnnaBell and I almost jumped out of our skin. "Zeila!" we gasped together, instantly terrified.

Witch Zeila was the most dangerous inhabitant of Croneswart Swamp. She and her eight-legged hut were famous. The hut walked. Zeila flew on a broom. Both struck terror in the hearts of good people.

Fortunately, the hut looked abandoned. It was empty except for the two halves of a broken broom lying in a corner. But of course I knew that empty didn't mean safe.

And looking empty didn't always mean empty.

"Nice place," AnnaBell remarked sarcastically, "but I wouldn't want to live—"

Skree-ee-eek!

Without warning, the hut shuddered and the shrieks of creaking gears filled the air. Then the whole building started to sway from side to side as if caught in an earth-quake.

"Get down!" I yowled, dragging AnnaBell to the floor.

Zeila's hut was doing exactly what it was supposed to do. It was walking across the swamp. And there was no telling when or where it would stop.

Which it didn't do for at least an hour.

When it finally stumbled to a stop, I pointed at the door and AnnaBell nodded eagerly. She wanted to escape as much as I did. So we scampered out in a rush, not too careful about bumping into each other along the way down.

"I never thought I'd be so happy to see the swamp!" she exclaimed. Like a kid at the beach, she was splashing playfully at the water's edge.

But I wasn't in such a good mood. I was listening to something, and it wasn't good news.

Fwum-fwum. Fwum-fwum.

The beating of the experiment had changed. It wasn't clear or strong anymore. It sounded muffled, as if it were buried or far away.

For a moment, I wondered why. But for only a moment. Seeing AnnaBell stomp and splash solved the riddle for me.

The experiment had gone underwater. It was deep beneath Croneswart Swamp.

36

For the next few minutes, I was a blur of activity. I pushed up my sleeves and sat down to do what I did best. Build gadgets. It was my time to shine, even while sitting in the mud.

AnnaBell watched with a curious look on her face. She'd never seen me in real action before.

Snickt! I fitted parts together. *Ernt, ernt, ernt!* I tightened bolts. *Kwit-kwit!* I snipped excess material.

"What are you making?" she finally asked.

The poor thing! I thought without pausing. *Can't she tell?*

The drivets, triddles, and thoozles were a dead giveaway. I was building S.A.M.B.U.'s—Swamp Air Masks for Breathing Underwater. It should have been obvious.

"Uh, it's a surprise," I said, not wanting to hurt AnnaBell's feelings. She clearly didn't know anything about gadgets, and I didn't want to rub it in.

"Fine!" she snorted. "Don't tell me. I'll just practice my juggling over here."

I stopped working that instant. My hands and fingers froze and my head shot up.

"No, don't," I said, more forcefully than I should have. "You're juggling is dangerous."

Then, to myself, I added, *It's also our secret weapon.* I planned on having her juggle when we caught up to the Spinasaurus Rex. She would freeze the monster, and I would nab the experiment in Wizard Ast's hat. Just like that, we'd be the newest heroes of Tiller's Field.

It sounded so simple. Too simple really, and I should have known better. The best things we do are usually the hardest. That's what makes them worth doing.

AnnaBell smirked at me, head titled to one side, hands on her hips. She was still trying to figure out what I was building.

"Ever hear the one about the girl who kept secrets from her friends?" she asked.

My back stiffened but I didn't stop working. *Not another joke,* I thought to myself. But out loud, I said, "Nope. Never heard it."

AnnaBell's smirk turned into a broad grin. "Pretty soon the girl didn't have any friends."

I waited, expecting more. The joke wasn't even close to funny. All of her others had been cheesy, not glum.

163

"Where's the punch line?" I finally asked. "Where's the 'bah-bah-boom'?"

"There isn't one," she shrugged. "It's a true story."

I crossed my eyes. "All right, I get it. I'm building masks so that we can breathe underwater. The Rex decided to go for a swim."

AnnaBell's face paled and her eyes darted to the swamp. "You want us to go after it?" she gasped. "In *there*?"

Instead of answering, I changed the subject. Letting AnnaBell think about the swamp was a bad idea. She might chicken out, and the thought of swimming alone terrified me.

"C'mere, I need your help," I said. "Put your finger here and push down."

For the next hour, we worked on our S.A.M.B.U.'s. AnnaBell's help made the job easier, and we finished in half the time it would normally take me.

When we were done, we strapped the masks over our faces.

AnnaBell took one look at me and started to laugh. "Your nose looks like a bog hog's," she snickered.

Which it did, I'm sure. The masks were tight, and they flattened our noses against our faces. But the good thing was that they each held about ten minutes of air.

"I wouldn't talk," I replied. "Your nose is a crooked bird beak."

She waved her hand carelessly, pretending to ignore my

comment. "Bog hog," she shot back quickly.

"Bird beak," I shot just as fast.

"Bog—" she started but her words turned into a shriek.

Gwo-o-o-sssh!

The swamp erupted like a volcano, drowning her voice and soaking us both. Chilly water, lily pads, and mud rained onto our heads. A terrifying roar accompanied the drenching.

Grr-rauwgh!

"Get back!" I cried, trying to push AnnaBell away from the shoreline.

She nimbly sidestepped me, digging in the pockets of her costume. Out came three juggling balls in the blink of an eye.

"Are you crazy?" I hollered at her. Now wasn't the time to fight. We weren't ready. We didn't have a plan.

But it was too late for that. The Spinasaurus Rex had sprung its trap, and we were caught. Instead of chasing the experiment, it had sneaked up on us.

Rusty buckets! I berated myself. *How could I have been so blind?* The Rex had been waiting in the water for us the whole time.

Standing knee-deep in the swamp, the monster towered over us—and most of the trees. Decaying, wet skin sagged from its bones like ribbons left out in the rain. In its chest the experiment blazed as brightly as ever.

Thwoon-thwoon! Thwoon-thwoon!

AnnaBell got her footing and tried to start juggling, but the Rex lashed out a rotting hand. Like a kid playing jacks, it easily scooped us off the ground. We barely had time to shriek.

The giant fist closed around us, and suddenly we lurched into the air. Between its fingers bones a blur of color rushed past, and then—

S-P-L-U-R-S-S-S-H!

Filthy water swallowed us, turning our cries into a flurry of bubbles. We were underwater and descending rapidly. The monster was dragging us down, down, down.

Would-be Hero

37

We sped deep into the murky gloom of Croneswart Swamp, prisoners of the Rex. My toes and fingers ached with cold. My eyes squinted as the light faded rapidly.

We were diving toward the bottom of the swamp, going where no human being belonged. I couldn't imagine being dry and warm ever again.

The light from the experiment cast strange shadows in the water. Slimy things with long squirmy bodies lurked just beyond its reach. They darted in the darkness like insects fleeing an overturned stone.

Finally I forced myself to look away. Peering into the shadows was frightening me, and I was frightened enough. Being dragged underwater by an undead monster did that to a person.

Where is the Rex taking us? I tried to puzzle it out. We had been underwater a long time. Had we not been wearing S.A.M.B.U.'s, we would have drowned already.

Thinking that, I guessed the Rex's plan. It wanted to drown us. That's why it had snatched us. Not to hold us prisoner but to kill us.

Lucky for us we could breathe underwater. For about five more minutes anyway.

A short distance ahead, the cavern curved into a sort of cave. Cut into its ceiling was a squarish hole like a window without shutters or glass. Dry land and sweet, sweet air waited beyond it.

We're saved! I wanted to shout. *Fresh air!*

I glanced at AnnaBell, full of hope. We weren't going to drown. I would build gadgets again. She—

Was out cold!

My heart leaped into my throat, and I felt sick. We were so close.

Air! Don't give up AnnaBell!

She was unconscious. Her head leaned limply to one side like a wilted flower. Her eyelids sagged almost all the way closed. No bubbles came from the tube attached to her mask.

So I took a huge breath and then did my impression of a hero-to-the-rescue. We could deal with the Rex later. AnnaBell's breathing was most important.

I clawed off her mask. Plastered mine over her face. Grabbed her collar. Set my feet. Exhaled. And slapped my scoot boots.

168

It all took a few seconds that seemed a lifetime long. My lungs shrieked for air. My limbs moved slowly, struggling against the current. Nothing I'd ever done had been more difficult.

Sploy – yoy – yoiiiiinnnggg!

My boot springs echoed dreamily, but the sound was the sound of success. Their powerful bounce broke open the Rex's fist and sent us speeding through the swamp like a harpoon.

We're free! I exulted. Maybe I really was a hero.

Flaumphf!

Then again, maybe not. I was so busy congratulating myself that I didn't see the wall coming. We smacked into solid rock at full speed. Ouch!

Amazingly, AnnaBell didn't stir. She slept on, a dead weight in my arms. Would anything wake her? I had doubts.

One thing at a time, Gidget, I reminded myself. *You've got to tighten the bolts before putting your weight on them.*

At that moment, I had to get AnnaBell and me out of the water. That was the first step. We needed air. Dry land, a safe place, awaken AnnaBell—in that order.

And try not to panic, I added.

But that was impossible. Over my shoulder, I saw the experiment getting ready to fire.

I shrieked bubbles and kicked my feet as if a shark were nipping at my toes. In the water, nowhere was safe.

38

S-s-s-splurgtt!

The experiment's blast brought Croneswart Swamp and everything in it to life. Light exploded. Heat swelled. AnnaBell gasped, coming awake.

Dark water churned white with bubbles. Waves raged, tossing us back and forth like bullies playing keep-away. They sent us sloshing, skimming, and soaring through—

"Air!" I cried, gulping the wind in my mouth. We were out of the swamp and into the tunnel. The experiment had saved us.

Thumph! Bomphf!

First me and then AnnaBell struck the ground like a wet pillow. Then we lay there with rocks poking into our backs, stunned and silent. We were too surprised to speak. We should have been dead.

We were in an underground passage large enough for the

Rex to walk along comfortably. The sound of dripping water echoed without. Clumps of fuzzy fungi clung to the rocky walls, glowing faintly.

"You all right?" I finally croaked, staring blankly at the ceiling. A long time had passed, and longer still before AnnaBell responded.

"*I*-I think so, Gidget" she stammered. Her voice sounded weak and far away.

That wasn't like AnnaBell. Her voice usually carried a smile or unspoken joke. Now she sounded like a different person.

"Is something—?" I started, rolling over to look at her. But the sight stole my voice, and I choked on my words.

"What?" she gasped, struggling anxiously to sit. "What is it?"

Eyes wide, I shook my head in disbelief.

"The experiment," I murmured. "It … changed you."

AnnaBell raised an arm that looked as thin as a flamingo's leg. Mud-colored splotches covered her skin. Frail fingers with swollen knuckles trembled uncontrollably.

"Oh, my," she sighed.

The experiment had aged her. Decades had been added to her life, maybe centuries. She was a living antique.

Her body was alarmingly frail. Grey hair sprouted from her head like twisted wire, and wrinkles marked her facial expressions. A breeze could probably scatter her limbs like dandelion seeds.

"I'm so sor—" I tried to apologize, but AnnaBell shook her head.

"We have to finish," she whispered, eyes closed. *"Beginning Is Unremarkable, Finishing a Masterpiece.* Help me up, please."

I marveled at her words and determination. The words came from *The Noble Deeds and Duties*, and they meant that starting something new was much easier than finishing.

Anyone could start to paint a picture, write a poem, assemble a puzzle, or save the world. But not everyone finished. Excuses and distractions usually got in the way.

Finishing was hard but always worth the effort. No one became a hero by starting something and then walking away before it was done.

That's easy for you to say, I told myself. *You haven't been turned into a living mummy like AnnaBell.*

I shuddered at the thought because it was true. The experiment and I were connected, but it hadn't harmed me yet. Was that on purpose or by accident?

Fwum-fwum. Fwum-fwum.

As if listening to my thoughts, the experiment suddenly let itself be heard again. It was still underwater but only for a moment more.

GWO-O-O-SSSH!

A crashing of waves and a terrible roar echoed through the tunnel. The moist stench of decay filled our nostrils.

Clumps of wet dirt plopped down from overhead.

"Help me!" ancient AnnaBell shrieked. "We have to run! Now!"

Her thoughts were mine exactly. The Rex had caught us again, and we still weren't ready to fight. We needed time to plan and catch our breath.

"Let's go!" I shouted, wrapping an arm around her waist. Immediately I noticed how thin and very light she felt.

There was only one direction to run in the tunnel. The Rex was behind us, dragging itself up out of the swamp. Ahead, the tunnel burrowed farther into the gloomy underground.

Hoping for the best, we started to shuffle down the passage. Whatever lay ahead couldn't be as bad as what lurked behind.

Dead Dead End

39

The tunnel seemed to go on forever. Patches of dimly glowing fungus lit our way. They cast eerie shadows and were the only change in scenery.

Everywhere else was damp rock. Rock and the endless thundering of the experiment.

Thwoon-thwoon! Thwoon-thwoon!

It had never sounded so loud, and it had never been so close for so long. The Rex was gaining on us.

Neither AnnaBell nor I turned around to look for it. There was no need. The Rex was somewhere behind, lumbering steadily on our trail. Pausing to look would only slow us down.

When we came to a fork in the tunnel, we paused. Two passages split away from the first, heading in different directions. We had a fast choice to make.

"Which way?" I asked, squinting right then left. "Can

you see anything?"

Peering into the new tunnels wasn't encouraging. Darkness filled them both. It was so thick that it seemed I should be able to touch it. Or that it should be able to touch me.

Suddenly I shivered uncontrollably. Something awful lurked in the darkness, something very old and very hungry. I couldn't see it, but that didn't make it less terrifying.

Problem was, I couldn't tell where it was exactly. Both tunnels gave me the same haunted feeling.

"Just pick one," AnnaBell whispered, leaning most of her weight against me. She weighed very little now, but I feared I would have to carry her if she leaned any farther.

She was still getting older, too. Her grey hair had turned white and was as thin as the silk on an ear of corn. Soon there would be nothing on her head but a soaking wet jester's cap.

We went left and the tunnel sloped downward almost immediately. But that didn't surprise me. Down was where it seemed we should go. Down to where the dead and buried waited.

By the time we'd taken a dozen steps, I really was carrying AnnaBell. The ground was too steep for her. She couldn't make it alone.

"Can you still juggle?" I asked, trying not to sound worried. It wasn't the most polite question, but at least I hadn't asked, *Are you too old to juggle?* That would have just been rude.

AnnaBell shivered against me, laughing or crying. I couldn't tell which, and she didn't make a sound.

"Does an ogre eat mushrooms?" she finally asked. "Do bog hogs melt in water?"

The answer to both questions was *yes*, of course. We'd seen the truth up close. So the answer to my question was the same. Despite being ancient, AnnaBell could still juggle.

"Bah-bah-boom!" she added softly.

I smiled at her and winked. *We might just win yet,* I thought jubilantly. Then we rounded a sharp corner and my hopeful feelings fell like dropped juggling balls.

We had reached a dead end, and the name had never been more appropriate. A *dead* dead end. That was where we were. It was no place for the living.

The tunnel widened into a massive cavern. Its ceiling arced into darkness, and one end of its floor dropped like a pit into a chasm. I'd never imagined a bigger place, nor one so filled with bones.

But these weren't just scattered bones, like pieces of an overturned puzzle. These bones were connected to one another. They formed dozens of giant skeletons.

"Rusty buckets," I gawked. We'd stumbled onto something horrifying, something that should never have been disturbed.

"It's like an elephant graveyard," AnnaBell hissed.

176

"For Spinasaurus Rexes," I finished.

To think, there had once been herds of the monsters roaming the land! One was bad enough.

"We have to get—" I tried to say, but the time for talk was over. We were dead-end dead.

Rumbling like an earthquake, the Spinasaurus Rex shambled around the corner and bellowed. The fireball in its chest darkened, preparing to fire.

"Run!" AnnaBell and I howled at the same time. Then we fled into the graveyard of dingy white bones.

40

"Over there!" AnnaBell rasped into my ear, pointing. "That's a good spot!"

We were half-running, half-sliding deeper into the cavern. Old bones poked up from the ground like roots in a dense forest. The chasm loomed ahead.

The bones frightened me more than anything. Not because they were the gruesome remains of monsters. Because the experiment could bring them back to life.

S-s-s-splurgtt! S-s-s-splurgtt!

Even now the Rex had its arms raised and the experiment was firing. But the blasts weren't aimed at us. They were striking the skeletons of the dead.

Bones rattled with life. They quivered and groaned, shaking sluggishly free from the earth. Tremors rumbled deep in the ground.

That's why the Rex is here, I realized. *To awaken more of its kind.*

And that was why we were here among the bones. To decide which way the future would go.

I scampered to where AnnaBell pointed. One giant hooked claw sprouted from the rocky ground nearby, but it was the only obstacle for a good stretch.

"Now what?" I shouted.

AnnaBell dug out her juggling balls.

"Hide behind that claw until these work," she told me, raising the balls. "Then do your thing, Gidget. I won't have much time."

Standing there without my support, she looked slimmer and older than ever. I didn't doubt that she had little time. She was less lively than the twitching skeletons.

"Just be careful," I said, backing up. It was a lame thing to say, but I couldn't think of anything else.

"Caution Is Bravery's Shield," she smiled, another of *The Noble Deeds and Duties.*

I nodded at her then crouched behind the claw, barely breathing. In one hand I clutched my slingshot. In the other, I gripped a stone. Wizard Ast's hat was tucked into my belt.

Maybe, just maybe, our plan was a good one.

A fiery blast of purple changed my thinking. We were in real trouble. The Rex had spotted us and was digging up reinforcements.

S-s-s-splurgtt!

The blast struck the claw near me and the gruesome thing came to life. Its fingers flexed and its wrist started to lash back and forth. A piercing screech like that of rusty gears filled the air.

I dove hard to my left, narrowly escaping the glowing bony claw. Fleshless fingers swiped at me blindly. Thank goodness they didn't have eyes!

Landing on a shoulder, I rolled and then vaulted to my feet. Gizmos clanked like broken glass in my backpack. I doubted that any of them still worked.

"Now, AnnaBell!" I cried, firing a stone at the claw with my slingshot. "Stop that thing!"

The Rex towered over us, a behemoth of bone and flesh and fur. It raised its arms and the experiment darkened. Another blast was on the way.

A blast that would make me a two-year-old. A blast that would turn AnnaBell into a fossil. A blast that—

Never came.

Finally I peeked my eyes open, afraid of what I'd see.

"Anna—?" I started before my friend cut me off.

"Your goggles!" she shouted. "Don't forget!"

I paused before lowering my goggles. "Thank you," I said softly. AnnaBell had just saved my life. Without her warning, I wouldn't have remembered.

"Uh huh," AnnaBell grunted. "Just hurry."

Suddenly I felt so proud. We'd done it! Defeated the Rex. All that was left was to slip the experiment into

Wizard Ast's hat.

But that was easier said than done, and I should have been wondering what could go wrong. Because after I took five steps, that was what happened. Everything went horribly wrong.

Five Steps

41

Five steps. That was all I took. Just five little steps. Then everything changed.

"Watch it!" AnnaBell hissed, desperate but unable to help.

Her juggling had frozen the Rex, and it would stay frozen for as long as she kept at it. But it hadn't frozen the claw and never would.

Why? It was simple. The claw was just a bony hand with fingers and nails. It didn't have eyes, and it couldn't see. It didn't even have eye sockets like the Rex.

No eyes meant no vision, and no vision meant no magic freeze. The claw was free to swat me. Which it did—*thwarnk!*—straight into AnnaBell.

The claw hit me. I hit AnnaBell. AnnaBell's juggling balls hit the ground. It was one-two-three.

Grr-Rauwgh!

Make that four. As soon as AnnaBell stopped juggling, the Rex exploded with movement. It bellowed and raised its arms, wasting no time.

S-s-s-splurgtt!

Out screeched a blazing bolt of molten purple. It struck AnnaBell square in the chest and spread like spilled paint, quickly enveloping her.

Next came my turn. The Rex wasn't taking chances or giving us any opportunity to escape. This time it would finish us before doing anything else.

S-s-s-splurgtt! A second bolt streaked my way. *S-s-s-splurgtt!* Then a third.

I leaped right then rolled left. Purple fire whisked past, prickling my skin. One wrong move, one step too slow—

S-s-s-splurgtt!

The fourth shot was a bull's eye. It hammered into my back and sent me flying.

"Rustyyyyyyyy—!" I yowled, legs and arms whirling. I was flying as if I'd been launched from my slingshot.

The chasm raced into view. So did something gooey, huge, and boggy brown.

It was a giant bog hog.

Sploosp!

I smacked into its side and stuck there like a snowball thrown against a wall. Cold slime plastered my mail and soaked my clothes. Nonuple yuck!

Then I slid down the side of the bog hog with an oozing

slowness and fell onto my back. The hog towered over me, as big as four of its kind.

"Hallo, leedle peeples," it said in a slobbery voice.

My eyes did a fast double-take. The hog hadn't spoken. Mougi had. He was sitting on the hog like a knight on a warhorse.

He grinned stupidly. "Mougi make big mud-pig like 'noman," he gurgled. "But it melt fas' in swamp."

I nodded automatically but didn't understand. A snowman was the last thing on my mind. But his hog did remind me of ice cream left out in the sun.

"Whatever you say," I agreed, then quickly changed the subject. "Can you see AnnaBell?" I still couldn't spot her among the piles of bones.

Mougi didn't answer. Directly ahead of him hunched a giant skeleton. Purple fire blazed in its eye sockets.

"Gid'yup!" the ogre bellowed, lowering his head and kicking his heels. But he wasn't turning or running away. He and the bog hog were heading straight for the skeleton.

Thwrangk!

Ogre, hog, and skeleton collided in a mighty muddy crash. Bones spun through the air like sticks tossed end over end. Clumps of sludge splattered the walls, the ceiling, and me.

Would I ever be clean again?

When the explosion cleared, the skeleton was gone. Stray bones lay scattered on the ground, still twitching, but not fitting together and standing back up.

But dozens of other skeletons shuffled about on stiff legs. Their joints creaked and popped, filling the air with unholy noise.

When one of them placed a chilling hand on my shoulder, I shrieked. My hands came up, swatting frantically as if I were in a cloud of stinging bees.

To my dismay, icy fingers snatched my wrists and refused to let go. Then things got really weird.

"Gidget, stop, it's me." AnnaBell's voice said.

I froze, staring dead into the eye sockets of a kid-sized skeleton. An *AnnaBell-sized* skeleton. The creepy thing was even wearing her hat.

Its cold fingers squeezed tighter. There was no pain in the grip, just an urgency.

"It's me," the skeleton repeated. "It's AnnaBell. Guess I finally knocked 'em dead. Bah-bah-boom."

My jaw fell open and my knees felt weak. The skeleton clutching my wrists wasn't just wearing AnnaBell's hat. It *was* AnnaBell. The experiment's last blast had done the unthinkable.

AnnaBell had been turned into one of the walking dead.

42

"I'll be all right," AnnaBell the skeleton promised. "I can still juggle."

Her jaw flapped opened and closed like an oiled hinge as she spoke, but she didn't have vocal cords or a tongue. Speaking should have been impossible.

"If … if you say so," I mumbled, unconvinced. AnnaBell was skin and bones without the skin. Decuple yuck! No way was I going to argue with her.

Besides, she remembered our plan. Juggle first, freeze next, hat last. She was ready to go.

She let go of my wrists and nodded, making the bells on her hat jingle. More than anything, their sound convinced me that she really was my friend.

And why not? In a roomful of skeletons, one of them could be friendly. I'd seen stranger things, like a friendly ogre riding a friendly bog hog.

S-s-s-splurgtt!

The Spinasaurus Rex launched blast after blast from the pulsing experiment. AnnaBell shuffled one way. I scampered the other. Mougi charged to the rescue.

"Up yous go," he burbled, catching my shoulders. Then he hauled me onto the bog hog's back, my legs spinning, still trying to run.

"Don't forget—!" I started to yell but a frightening sensation cut me short. My stomach flew up and the rest of me flew down. The world was tilting out of control.

G-R-O-I-N-K!

Beneath us, the bog hog squealed and reared like a spooked stallion. Its front hooves whirled over its head, spraying water and mud in gooey streamers.

"Down, piggy, whoa!" Mougi tried uselessly.

Two skeletons as tall as trees grasped at us with bony claws. More lumbered toward us. Others struggled to pull themselves up out of the earth.

Up out of their graves, I shivered, feeling sick. There was no end to the skeletons or the horror.

What a nightmare this was! What a mistake! Skeletons weren't supposed to come to life. The dead were supposed to stay dead. Didn't they know that?

S-s-s-splurgtt!

Another fiery shot answered my question. The Spinasaurus Rex didn't care that it was supposed to be dead. The skeletons didn't care either. All of them would kill us to stay alive.

We were in a fight to the finish.

"Yah!" I roared, jabbing my heels into the bog hog's squishy sides. The beast squealed again, dropping to all fours. Another jab got it running.

Thwrangk!

We bowled into a skeleton, taking it square in the shins. Its legs went one way, its body the other. We galloped beneath both and raced on.

S-s-s-splurgtt! S-s-s-splurgtt!

Purple fired blazed wildly. It sizzled like bacon in a skillet and made my hair stand on end. Streak after streak hurtled toward us like flaming spears.

Somehow the bog hog dodged them all. First left, then right, then with a perfectly timed leap. The experiment couldn't touch us, and we were closing in.

Thwoon-thwoon! Thwoon-thwoon! Thwoon—!
WHOOLM!

The ground exploded in a sudden blinding flash. The bog hog squealed and somersaulted into a hole that hadn't been there seconds before. Mougi and I were thrown helplessly through the air.

No, the experiment couldn't touch us. But it could touch the ground in front of us. In fact, it could blow it to smithereens.

Thamp! THOMP!

First I landed, then Mougi. I hit the ground. He hit me.

Rusty buckets, how I wished it could have been the other way around.

"Get ... off," I wheezed, pushing with all my might. There were enough monsters trying to crush me. Mougi didn't need to help.

"Yous is too bony for a pillow," he told me seriously and rolled over.

"Too bony?" I shrieked when I was free. "Too bony! Have you seen AnnaBell?"

Without thinking, I jumped up and pointed at my skeleton friend. Now she was too bony. She was *all* bony. And at the moment, she was also—

Juggling.

Seeing that, I froze. So did Mougi and the Rex. So did the army of undead. AnnaBell was all that moved in the cavern. She was all that could.

One Horror For Another

43

"Oh, don't look at me like that," AnnaBell sassed. "You're not frozen. You're wearing goggles."

My hands shot instantly to my head. What a knucklehead! My goggles were still covering my eyes. I'd forgotten again that they protected me from her juggling.

At least I hadn't had time to take them off.

I grinned sheepishly. "Just testing you," I muttered, forcing a chuckle.

AnnaBell kept juggling but turned to look at me. If she'd had lips, I was sure they would have been smirking.

"You're supposed to leave the jokes to me, remember?" she stated flatly.

"I never agreed to that," I shrugged. "Bah-bah-boom." Then I made a face and AnnaBell snickered.

We were playing, of course. Neither of us was really mad. We had beaten the Rex and were on our way to becoming heroes. What was there to be upset about?

Skurzzzk!

Turns out there was plenty. Danger was getting ready to pounce on us again.

"*G*-Gidget?" AnnaBell whispered. This time her voice wasn't flat. It quaked with fear.

I swallowed hard and nodded, turning slowly. I'd heard the cracking, buzzing noise, too. It had sounded electric. Only one thing in the cavern could make a noise like that.

The experiment.

"Get down!" I shouted, diving for cover.

We'd made a mistake, I realized. A terrible, deadly mistake. We'd forgotten that the experiment didn't have eyes. It couldn't be stopped by AnnaBell's juggling.

Guh-Whooolm!

A thunderous blast shook the cavern. Skeletons collapsed, rocks were flattened, and the experiment burst free. Shrieking wind hurled AnnaBell and I backward as if we were straw hats.

Surprisingly, we landed very close to one another. AnnaBell clanked like a dropped sack of nails. I made a wet thump, then saw stars.

"Roll!" she hissed sharply.

Her eye sockets blazed orange, so I obeyed without question. When a skeleton looked at me that way, I thought it best to listen.

Whooolm!

The experiment crashed between us. It churned like a tornado, spitting lightning and belching thunder. Behind it, the Rex crumbled into a heap of glittering dust.

I realized then that the experiment had changed. It wasn't the same fireball that had escaped Wizard Ast's castle. Now it was a violent storm more deadly than any monster.

We've traded one horror for another, I told myself. The Rex was gone. Its skeletons were sinking back into their graves. But the experiment was loose, wild, and hungry.

As we watched, it started to roll and quickly build up speed. Rocks, bones, and AnnaBell's balls tumbled into it, drawn like metal to a magnet. All were devoured in violet flames.

"It's growing!" AnnaBell cried, grasping my hand. The stiff chill of her bony fingers didn't frighten me as much as the experiment.

That was because she was right. The experiment was growing. Whatever it swallowed made it bigger, and it swallowed everything in its path.

Already it was the size of a horse-drawn carriage, horses and driver included. What would stop it from getting as big as a Spinasaurus Rex?

Immediately I answered my own question. *We will,* I thought, knowing that we had made the decision long ago. That was why we were here—to stop the experiment.

AnnaBell gasped as the experiment rolled over the edge

of the chasm and into the valley below. There were tunnels down there, some that probably led to the surface. If it escaped now, there would be no stopping it later.

But I ignored all that. My mind was elsewhere. I was busy designing the gadget that would stop the experiment once and for all.

44

"Bones!" I barked like a general on a battlefield. "I need bones, all different sizes. And Mougi's vest. Hurry!"

Now that AnnaBell had stopped juggling, Mougi was his old drooling self again. He lumbered toward me with a bubbly smile on his face. His bog hog had melted into a muddy puddle.

"Why yous want Mougi shirt?" he gurgled. "It too big for leedle peeples."

I opened my mouth to answer, but quickly snapped it shut. The real explanation would have been too complex. I had to keep it simple.

"It's a surprise," I said, which was true. I hadn't heard of anyone building an Ogre Fling-Launched Aerial Pursuit (O.F.L.A.P., for short) before. That made it a surprise.

"Here," AnnaBell said, dropping an armload of loose bones at my feet. "Need more?"

194

She asked casually, as if wondering whether I wanted more sticks for a campfire. As if picking up monster bones were normal and everyday.

I smiled at her, feeling proud of all of us. We were a lot tougher than I ever would have guessed. Wizard Ast would be pleased. I sure was.

For the next several minutes, I concentrated on building my new gadget. I used a dozen bones, Mougi's vest, and a handful of gizmos. I was grateful that my dad's handiwork had survived being tossed around in my backpack.

I finished in record time then stood up to admire my work. The O.F.L.A.P. resembled a large pair of bat wings and was as long as Mougi was tall.

"What is it?" AnnaBell asked immediately. Mougi just squinted and scratched his head.

"An O.F.L.A.P.," I replied. "An Ogre Fling-Launched Aerial Pursuit. I'm going to fly down and capture the experiment."

AnnaBell's jaw *clacked* as it dropped open. "Not without me, you're not," she protested.

I could have argued but didn't. AnnaBell and I had started our mission by flying after the experiment together. We should finish it the same way.

"Just hang on tight and don't let go when we're in the air," I told her.

She batted one of the bells on her cap in annoyance. "I'm the jester," she muttered. "No more jokes from you."

Mougi interrupted before a real argument could start. "Where does Mougi hang on?"

I shook my head. "You don't. You have a more important job." The *fling* part of the job. "You're going to throw us."

Silence followed. Mougi drooled slowly and AnnaBell stared, frozen with surprise. Thankfully neither of them accused me of joking.

Before they got moving or talking again, I looped the O.F.L.A.P.'s straps over my shoulders. I'd cut them off my backpack. Then I struggled to stand. No way could I walk with the wings on my back.

AnnaBell cocked her head at me. "Not your best look," she commented. "Maybe a nice pair of earrings would look better."

I smirked. "How about no more jokes from you either?" I suggested breathlessly. "But a little help would be nice."

AnnaBell skipped lightly over to me and put her skeletal weight against my shoulders.

"I can't make any promises," she said. "My brother uses spells to make magic. I use jokes."

I shut my mouth. How could I argue with that?

Mougi picked us up next and carried us to the edge of the chasm.

"Buh-bye," he grinned sloppily.

Here comes the fling, I dreaded.

Then the ogre roughly tossed us off the edge of the chasm

as if he were playing a game of king-of-the-hill. AnnaBell and I screamed and watched his flat face shrink as we fell.

Distract for the Hat

45

Falling fast, we screamed until—

S-s-s-splurgtt!

—the experiment attacked and barely missed.

Hot wind swept over us. Light blazed behind my eyelids. Then the O.F.L.A.P.'s wings caught some air, straightened, and started to fly.

"Lean to the right!" I shouted to AnnaBell. *S-s-s-splurgtt!* "Now to the left!" *S-s-s-splurgtt!*

Fiery bolts shrieked past on both sides. Only by leaning did we dodge the attacks, but that wouldn't work forever. We were too unprotected in the air.

Rusty buckets, Gidget! I berated myself. *You sure didn't think this through.*

I had assumed that the experiment would try to escape. I'd planned on sneaking up on it. But it had surprised us. It had waited for us like a cat poised outside a mouse hole.

S-s-s-splurgtt!

"Rusty buckets!" I repeated out loud. "We have to land or that thing will blast us out of the sky!"

I was angry with myself. My plan had seemed so clever. Soar into the chasm, lower Wizard Ast's hat, and scoop up the experiment like a pelican snatching a fish. I hadn't thought that the experiment would have time to fight back.

"I have an idea," AnnaBell said quickly. "You keep flying. I'll take my act to the ground."

Less than a second passed before I realized what she meant. She was going to jump.

"No!" I cried. "That's not the plan! You'll be—!"

S-s-s-splurgtt!

Another shot from the experiment cut me off. We leaned hard to the right again, and then AnnaBell let go.

Well, I called it letting go. She would have called it jumping.

"AnnaBell!" I shrieked.

Down she fell, faster than I thought possible. Her bony white arms whirled and her hat jingled. Not once did she scream or cry out, not even when she hit the ground in a perfect bellyflop.

Floonk!

But she did hop to her feet afterward as if she'd landed on pillows instead of rocks.

"I'm fine!" she shouted up to me, tapping the side of her skull. "I'm all bones and no brains!"

Bones can break, you knucklehead, I thought to myself. *And so can brains!*

I couldn't decide which I felt more. Anger at AnnaBell for letting go or relief that she was all right.

Was that how my parents felt when they caught me doing something dangerous? They had hugged and scolded me at the same time more than once.

S-s-s-splurgtt!

The experiment didn't give me time to figure that out. It struck quickly, almost forcing me to let go to avoid being hit.

I leaned hard and banked left, screaming as flames whisked past. Heat warmed the bottom of my feet, even through my sturdy scoot boots.

The experiment was almost directly beneath me, and that wasn't as far away as it should have been. Since we'd seen it last, it had kept growing. Now it was as big as the frog statue outside Castle Ninespire.

How am I was supposed to fit that into Wizard Ast's hat? I pondered. No wonder I trusted gadgets more than magic.

S-s-s-splurgtt! S-s-s-splurgtt!

Two more blasts lashed out, too fast for me to dodge them both. I was hit! Fire engulfed my right wing, setting its bones alight.

If you're going to do something, do it now, I silently encouraged AnnaBell. *I don't have much time left.*

Astonishingly, AnnaBell came through at exactly the puff

right time.

Flid-deh-dit!

A handful of playing cards zipped from her hand toward the experiment. She must have been saving them for an emergency, and I couldn't think of a better time.

"My five-card straight will seal your fate!" she shouted.

I had hoped for something incredible to happen. Something explosive and loud. But the cards struck and were instantly incinerated.

"You're going to get yourself killed!" I cried, disappointed.

S-s-s-splurgtt! S-s-s-splurgtt!

Fire streaked quickly at AnnaBell but she dodged quicker. Bones creaking, she cartwheeled inches ahead of the blazing attacks.

"Your spark is worse than your smite!" she mocked, bounding to her feet and tossing another card.

S-s-s-splurgtt!

The experiment fired at her again, forgetting about me. AnnaBell was closer and being annoying. I knew how it felt!

That's it! I finally understood. The cards and her antics weren't meant to hurt. They were meant to annoy.

AnnaBell was distracting the experiment so that it would leave me alone.

"Is that the best you can do?" she continued to taunt. Then in baby talk, she added, "Why, you're jus' a widdle puff o' smoke."

Hearing that, the experiment darkened. Purple flames deepened to black. Punishing blasts streaked from it nonstop.

S-s-s-splurgtt! S-s-s-splurgtt!

"Now, Gidget!" AnnaBell shouted over her shoulder. "Hurry!"

My heart swelled with gratitude. *Thank you!*

Grunting with effort, I threw all of my weight right. The O.F.L.A.P. jerked, bounced, and then looped into a tight spiral.

Suddenly I was spinning downward like water rushing into a narrow drain. Wind tore my goggles from my face. It took both of my hands to keep a grip on Wizard Ast's hat.

I'm never going to make it, I thought in a panic. *I'm going to crash into the fire.*

Rocks whirled crazily below me. Flames blazed everywhere. For one blurry second I spotted AnnaBell, still leaping and twisting. Then she vanished in the confusion.

"Rusty bucketsssssssssss!" I wailed.

I really thought I was going to die.

Then—*fwooosh!*—the O.F.L.A.P. miraculously caught another jet of air. For a split second it hovered inches above the experiment.

I was so close to I could lay my palm on it.

So I did. Just about.

With both hands, I lowered Wizard Ast's hat and stretched

it open as wide as I could. I felt silly doing it because I still didn't completely trust magic. The hat was a fraction of the size of the experiment. But what choice did I have?

B-B-B-BLOOOONG!

Without warning, everything exploded at once. The hat, the experiment, the fire, even AnnaBell. But instead of flying apart, it all seemed to shrink.

The explosion's terrible stinging light forced me to squeeze my eyes shut.

Bah-Bah-Boom!

46

When I opened my eyes, I expected to see smoke and ash. I thought the whole cavern would be scorched and black.

It wasn't. It was empty.

Sure, I saw dirt and rocks and even a couple of mushrooms growing here and there. But that was it. Everything else was gone. Including AnnaBell.

"AnnaBell!" I shrieked. I waited, listening. Then I shrieked again and again.

She was gone, just like the experiment. Both had disappeared in the shrinking explosion. Both had been swallowed by Wizard Ast's hat.

My voiced cracked, but I didn't give up. I dug furiously in the hat. I tipped it upside down and shook it.

Nothing fell out, not even a speck of lint.

"Anna … Bell …" I sobbed. She was really gone.

From there, I stumbled around the cavern in a daze. I wasn't going anywhere in particular. I was lost and exhausted.

At some point I ran into Mougi, but I hardly recognized him. Tears and fatigue had nearly blinded me. The ogre must have climbed down to rescue us ... *me.*

He picked me up, and I remember little else of our journey to Tiller's Field. Just the dreams I had of running blind in a snowstorm. Even in sleep I was lost.

I woke to a crowd of faces staring at me. My parents were there, along with my little brother. For once he wasn't making any noise or demands.

Lots of other people I knew where there, too. Little Jozlyn, Simon, Wizard Ast, Mougi, the sheriff, his deputy, and more.

Only one face was missing. A tiny face with a big smile. The face that belonged to my friend AnnaBell.

Thinking of her, I groaned. My eyes rolled back and started to close.

"Oh, no, you don't, young lady," Wizard Ast chided softly. He was still a kid with a beard but talked like an adult. "Stop-desist right there."

I looked into his bright eyes and he smiled. The look told me that he had a secret.

"Your quest-mission is not complete," he whispered.

Just leave me alone, I thought, too tired to speak. *Haven't I done enough already?*

Apparently I hadn't, because Mougi picked me up and carried me outside. Everyone else followed.

We were in the center of town, and it was packed with people. They lined the streets as if waiting for a parade to stroll by. Every citizen of Tiller's Field must have been there.

The crowd, however, couldn't hide the fact that the entire town was in ruins. Flattened houses still smoked from recent fires. Too many children and not enough adults stood in the crowd.

The experiment, I lamented. *It destroyed so much.*

Mougi set me on my feet, and the crowd went dead silent. Then a little boy scurried into the street and pointed at me. His face was rosy with excitement, and he wore goggles over his eyes.

"That's her, Mommy!" he squealed. "That's Tinker Gidget the Hero!"

My jaw dropped open at that. *Hero?* I'd gotten my friend killed. The sheriff should have been arresting me. I wasn't a hero.

But to my surprise, the crowd cheered. They cheered, applauded, and chanted my name. Many of them waved goggles over their heads.

It was ridiculous!

"But …" I tired to protest, raising my hands. The crowd cheered louder at the gesture.

Finally I looked to Wizard Ast. He was sitting on

Mougi's shoulders now. When he lifted his hands, the crowd quieted.

I expected a speech next. It just felt like that kind of moment. Instead, the wizard reached dramatically into his robes like a magician on stage.

Or a jester performing a trick.

Oh, AnnaBell! I'm sorry!

He pulled out his floppy hat and the crowd went berserk with applause. He didn't have to say a word.

When he dipped a hand into the hat, silence instantly returned. Even I held my breath.

Time is free.
Time is wild.
Time is a playful-impish child.

he chanted.

Time is now.
Time is here.
Time is a friendship-ally dear.

Time is short.
Time is brief.
Time is a stealthy-cunning thief.

Time is past.
Time is gone.
Time is a fading-waning dawn.

Then he quickly pulled the hat inside-out and tossed it high into the air. There it twirled in place, slowly at first but quickly gaining speed.

Purple sparks the size of snowflakes sprang from the hat. They twinkled like fireworks and slowly drifted downward in a dazzling blizzard. Soon a glowing blanket settled in over the town.

And everywhere it lay magic happened.

Children aged, growing up again. Houses straightened, reformed, and stood tall. Color repainted everything that had been burned.

Tiller's Field was being healed before our eyes. Castle Ninespire would surely be repaired in the same way later.

Soon the Spinasaurus Rex would be a memory. So would the experiment.

And so will AnnaBell, I couldn't help thinking. My friend was gone, and no glowing purple snow could bring her back.

Head down, I turned and started to walk slowly away. The rest of the townsfolk played and celebrated. They tossed purple snowballs, made purple snow angels, and slipped around on their shoes like ice skaters.

Oddly, only one little group was building a snowman. It was led by a grown-up Wizard Ast. I almost ran into him before looking up.

When I did, I realized my mistake. The group wasn't building a snowman. They had finished a snow*girl*. On her head was a belled jester's cap.

"AnnaBell?" I gasped, my throat tightening.

As I watched, the snowgirl started to melt. Purple water dripped rapidly down her hat, her face, her body, and legs. Soon she was a shivering, soaking wet, real live girl.

"AnnaBell!" I cried again. "Is it really you?"

She winked at me and tilted her wet head, bells jingling.

"Who did you expect—Frosty the Snowman?" she giggled. "Bah-bah-boom!"

The End

Knightscares Adventures

#1: Cauldron Cooker's Night
#2: Skull in the Birdcage
#3: Early Winter's Orb
#4: Voyage to Silvermight
#5: Trek Through Tangleroot
#6: Hunt for Hollowdeep
#7: The Ninespire Experiment

More Adventures Coming Soon!

Want Free Knightscares ?

Join the Official Knightscares Fan Club Today!

Visit www.knightscares.com

Read the latest conjurings, spells, and news from the co-wizards, David and Charlie.

*Join the Free Fan Club
Get Your Name on the Knightscares Website
Preview Upcoming Adventures
Invite the Authors to Your School
Lots More!*

Discover More Adventure
in
Knightscares #8

Never Make a Deal With a Dragon

Noah and his sister Naomi think they have problems. When bullies chase them into the deadly needlespine pines, one loud noise could be their last.

A boy named Ian rescues them, but he has troubles of his own. He has been turned into a werewolf by a terrible curse.

To break the curse, the kids set off across the frozen wastes of Neverthaw, land of ice and storm. They hope to make a deal with a dragon. But dragons are cunning and their deals always have a price.

Knightscares #8

Visit
www.knightscares.com
for more information

Noble Deeds and Duties found in The Ninespire Experiment

When There Is No One Else, There Is Still You.

The Heart of a Hero Is Not Measured By Size.

Caution is Bravery's Shield.

Beginning Is Unremarkable, Finishing a Masterpiece.

Hone Friendship Until It Is Stronger Than Armor and Reaches Farther Than a Sword.

Loyalty Cannot Be Proven Too Often.

Knightscares Artwork Winners

All three artists will receive a free autographed copy of Knightscares #7: The Ninespire Experiment.

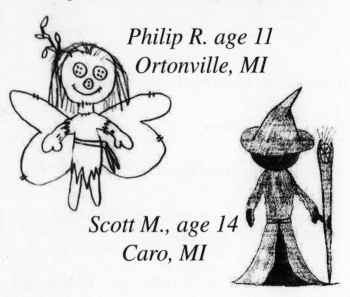

Philip R. age 11
Ortonville, MI

Scott M., age 14
Caro, MI

Nastasja R., age 11
Cumberland, RI

Knightscares Artwork Winners

*Sarah E.,
Age 11
Rockford,
MI*

Send Your Drawings to:
Knightscares Artwork
P.O. Box 654
Union Lake, MI   48387

*Find out about the Knightscares Fan Art Contest at
www.knightscares.com*

Thank you, Artists! Great job!

The Ninespire Experiment Artwork

The hand-painted cover art, official Knightscares logo, maps, and interior illustrations were all created by the talented artist Steven Spenser Ledford.

Steven is a free-lance fine and graphic artist from Charleston, SC with nearly 20 years experience. His work includes public and private wall murals, comic book pencil, ink and color, magazine illustrations and cover art,   t-shirt designs, sculptures, portraits, painted furniture and more. Most of his work is produced from the tiny rooms of the house he shares with his very patient wife and their two children—Xena (a psychotic tortoise-shell cat) and Emma (a Jack Russell terrier). He welcomes inquiries at PtByNmbrs@aol.com.

Thank you, Steven!